Bait
for
a Tiger

by

BAYARD VEILLER

Author of "Within the Law,"
"The Trial of Mary Dugan,"
etc.

CRESTWOOD PUBLISHING CO., INC.
NEW YORK · 1943

BLACK CAT DETECTIVE SERIES

IT is the aim of the Publishers to bring to the public from time to time, inexpensive editions of better detective mystery novels to be known as the BLACK CAT DETECTIVE SERIES.

THIS mystery thriller was originally published by *Reynal & Hitchcock* at $2.00.

WILDSIDE PRESS

www.wildsidepress.com

CHAPTER 1

THE first of the murders, that of Maggie Cort, attracted very little attention. After all, what is one girl more or less? The police, under Captain Edward Wilson of the Homicide Squad, investigated. There was nothing very horrible about the sight of Maggie as she lay dead. Just a thin, golden-haired girl lying on the sidewalk in front of her own home, a tenement on East 93rd Street. Dr. Singleton, the medical examiner, reported that she had been stabbed through the heart with a thin-bladed knife used by a practiced hand. Here is what he said about it: "The work might have been done by a doctor. A swift thrust with this two-edged knife, a twist of the wrist, and the heart was sliced to ribbons. So almost no blood came from the body.

"And that," said Dr. Singleton, "is the sign of a skilled workman."

The reporter to whom he was talking looked at him with a grin and said: "Can you describe the murderer?"

"Yes," said Dr. Singleton. "I can. He had two arms, two legs, one nose and a couple of ears, or it may have been a woman with only one ear."

"That," said the reporter, "doesn't tell me very much."

"Listen, son," said old Singleton. "If you want facts come to me for them. If you want theories, there are a lot of bookstores up on Fourth Avenue. Read Edgar Wallace or Philip McDonald or some of those birds."

But there was one thing about this case the police didn't give to the reporters, something that sharply aroused police interest. It was important because it was the reason Captain Wilson and not some other detective officer was put in charge of the investigation; but otherwise it didn't turn out to be of

3

much use. It was a single sheet of soiled paper on which a much-used typewriter had set down the following:

Mr. Commissioner,

I never saw this girl before. She is dead because your department is rotten and I want to show you how rotten it is. There are plenty of bad cops in it. The worst of all is Captain Wilson. Get rid of him and all the other bad ones or you will find more dead girls. Don't waste time trying to trace me. I used gloves fixing up this letter and you won't find any fingerprints. You'll never catch me anyhow because I'm too smart for your whole darn lousy department.

This letter was taken to Commissioner Doyle at once and Captain Wilson was in the Commissioner's office a few moments later. Wilson was one of the most respected men in the department, a man with a fine record; naturally angered by the attack on him, he asked the Commissioner to put him in charge of the case, and the Commissioner readily agreed. Wilson could think of no reason why he should thus be singled out by the murderer; the letter sounded as if it had been written by a crank with a fancied grievance, but search his memory as Wilson would he could think of no one whom he could fit into the picture as the probable criminal.

So little Maggie Cort was buried. There weren't many people to remember her. Her mother, of course, and the boy she was to have married.

Maggie would have been forgotten entirely if it hadn't been for Sarah Drake. Maggie was blonde, Sarah was dark. Maggie was slim, Sarah was plump. But three days after they had laid Maggie in her grave they found Sarah Drake ready for hers — found her just a couple of blocks from where they'd found Maggie. Commissioner Doyle called Captain Wilson in to talk about it.

"Got any theories?" he asked.

Captain Wilson snorted. "Theories? Hell! Doc Singleton says one fellow did both murders. All right, I'll believe him. But what are you going to do about a man who leaves no fingerprints, no marks, nothing?"

"We'll have to find him, you know," said Police Commissioner Doyle.

"Yes, I know and I will find him. But, Commissioner, we're up against it. There are no clues. Just a plain case of blood lust plus what looks like a grudge against me and the rest of your department."

Doyle got up from his desk and went over to where Wilson was standing looking out of the window at the hurrying crowds along Centre Street. The window was up and the roar of traffic swept in. Here were two men who had worked together for years. They had been roundsmen together and Doyle, because of his greater ability or perhaps greater political pull, had become Police Commissioner and Wilson only a captain. But there was a quarter of a century of close association between them. For a minute Doyle stood beside the Captain and they both looked at the city below them.

"Pretty tough, isn't it, Ed?" said Doyle.

"Yes," said the Captain.

"I can't help thinking what I would do if it was my Kitty. She's just about the age of that Cort girl and she's a little yellow-haired thing too."

Wilson turned on him with a shout. "For God's sake shut up!" Then he got hold of himself. "Sorry, Commissioner."

Doyle rested his hand lightly on the other's shoulder. "That's all right, Ed. You've got a girl too, and I'm her godfather. I know how you feel about this business for I feel the same way."

Captain Wilson turned squarely toward his superior. "All right, Commissioner, I guess we'll have to get that fellow."

Doyle looked at him for a moment and then waved to a chair. He himself sat on the edge of his desk and looked down at his old friend.

"Ed, we've learned a lot about police work in twenty-five years, haven't we? We can do almost everything. We can take charred and shattered paper and put it together again and bring out what was written on it. We can take smudges and develop them into fingerprints. We use chemistry in the most extraordinary and exciting ways. But there is one thing we have never learned, and that is to read the mind of an insane man.''

"So,'' said Wilson, "what's the use of all this? There have been a couple of murders exactly alike within three or four days in my precinct. They've been done by a crazy man — or maybe a crazy woman. How are you going to tell? Eventually I'll find out. But not now — unless by accident. Perhaps some passerby might by the merest chance witness the next murder.''

Doyle looked startled. "You think there'll be more? There'll be another murder?''

"Certainly there'll be another murder. That's awful, isn't it? I hope when he kills again he will do some one thing that will give us something to work on.''

"What about the dead girls?'' asked the Commissioner. "Their friends, their companions? You know what I mean.''

"Good as gold,'' said Wilson. "Hard-working, decent, lived at home, turned in their money to their families, went with nice boys. You couldn't ask for two nicer girls. And just slaughtered, that's what they were, slaughtered.'' The two men looked at each other in silence.

Said Doyle, "You talked to the Medical Examiner. What had he to say? What's his theory?''

"He hasn't any,'' said Wilson. "He has this fact for us. He said that in no case would there be any bloodstains on the hands or clothes of the murderer, because no blood would spurt. He says the murder, the whole thing — the killing, the walking away from the body — could have been done in less than a minute. Just a plunge of the knife, a twist of the wrist, dropping the body on the sidewalk, and walking away. He would not commit himself as to whether the man who did it was a doctor or not. He said the person who did it had had practice, knew where to plunge the knife and how to cut the human heart to pieces with a twist of the wrist. We could put extra men in plain clothes on certain streets at night. But what good would that do? They tried that in London years ago with the Jack the Ripper cases. English policemen were falling all over each other, but they never found anything. But it's equally true that we can't sit still and let this matter rest. Something's got to be done.''

CHAPTER 2

IF THE CROOKS HAD ONLY KNOWN IT, that night would have been a wide-open time for them in the section of the city in which the bodies of Maggie Cort and Sarah Drake had been found. With the exception of the men on fixed posts — and in this part of town there were very few — every man had a special assignment. From two o'clock in the afternoon till ten o'clock that night, without interruption, with no time for rest, no time for meals, each policeman went from house to house, apartment to apartment. And the first question was: Have you a daughter in your home? And the second was: How old is she? And if there was a daughter anywhere from sixteen to thirty, there was this special message from the Captain. If any man she doesn't know begins to speak to her she is to start screaming first and then to run. That was all they had to do — scream, run, scream. Keep on screaming. Captain's orders.

At ten o'clock that night Meyer Solomon came running into the station house. What he wanted was a policeman, he didn't care if it was a captain, a sergeant, or a lieutenant. He wanted a policeman. What did he want him for, asked a sergeant. ''I got a dead girl in my pushcart!'' cried Solomon.

He got several policemen. There were Captain Wilson, a couple of lieutenants and a sergeant. Under the rags of the cart they found the body of a girl. No bloodstains, nothing. So the cart was picked up and carried into the station and the owner dragged after it. He couldn't explain anything. He had left his cart in an alleyway while he went to eat, and when it was time to go home he found it heavy. And he thought boys had been playing tricks on him. That is when he pulled back the rags and paper and stuff out of which he made his living, and found the body of Caroline Hazzard. She was a little thing, a hunchback. Wilson stood looking down at the body a minute and then without speaking went into the office and phoned Doyle. The Police Commissioner phoned the Mayor and there was a secret meeting that night in the City Hall — Wilson and the Mayor and Police Commissioner Doyle. They talked for an hour and got nowhere.

Captain Wilson had a possible explanation. It was founded, this theory of his, on the fact that all three murders had apparently been done by the same man, a man who had attacked him personally in a letter to the Commissioner. He gave voice to his thought after a great deal of talk had taken place. The Mayor, never a reserved man, was tramping up and down the floor of his office and raging. Doyle had tried to restrain him. His nerves were on edge too.

"Ego," raged the Mayor, "that's what it is, exaggerated ego, and silly as hell. Say it again, I want to be sure I heard you right the first time."

Wilson's face was red. "I told you it was only a theory."

"Yes," said Doyle quietly, "and yelling won't do any good."

"What's that?" shouted the Mayor.

"I said there was no use in your yelling at us," yelled Doyle, whose knowledge of the Mayor was profound. "I for one felt the need of your brains or we wouldn't be here."

"Oh," said the suddenly placated little man, "I see. If you boys will stop yelling at me perhaps we can get somewhere. Your theory, Captain, is that some crank is trying to make trouble for the department but particularly for you. It's a challenge to your ability; he's holding you up to public scorn. Is that it?"

"Yes," said Wilson, "that's about what I mean, only it's more than holding me up to public scorn, as you call it, sir. Unless I'm able to stop these murders and stop them by arresting the murderer it's going to cost me my job."

And then the door was opened — no one knocked, there had

been no warning — and a white-faced secretary, a man about twenty-six, edged into the room.

"What is it? I told you I wasn't —"

"There's a crazy man on the phone, your Honor, and he's laughing his head off. He says he's the man who's been killing those girls. And he wants to talk to you."

Doyle was at the door by that time. "I'll have that call traced — maybe we can get him." And he disappeared.

Wilson started to follow his chief. "Sit where you are," said the Mayor. "Take that extension and listen in."

"Yes," said the Mayor's urbane voice into the phone, "and what can I do for my constituent tonight? By the way, how did you find out I was here?"

"I followed that lousy Wilson down to your office and saw him go in there."

"Oooooh," said the Mayor, "I see. So you don't like Captain Wilson?" There was a pause. And if anything the Mayor's voice became even more tender. "I can't understand that," he said. "Wilson is a very popular man; everybody seems to like him. Most thorough and efficient officer we have. What have you against the man? No, of course you don't have to tell me unless you want to. Just why did you call me up?" All this in a quiet and somewhat uninterested tone.

From the extension phone this is what Captain Wilson heard after that; the voice was a high-pitched whisper:

"I thought you might like to put an end to all this killing of young girls."

"Yes," said the Mayor, "I'd like that very much."

"Then," said the voice, "let's make a deal. Kick Wilson out of the police; disgrace him. The fellow should have been broken years ago. Do it now."

The Mayor's face was purple. "Buy why, why, that's what I want to know."

Wilson's hand went over the transmitter of his phone. "That's right, sir, keep him talking. We'll get him. Just keep him talking."

The Mayor nodded at Wilson and went on with his conversation: "You give me any evidence against Wilson and I'll prefer charges. Surely a man of your intelligence knows I must have some definite reason. Give that reason, that's a good chap. Give me a reason."

The voice at the other end of the wire broke and rose to a scream. "Ask Wilson, ask Wilson, ask Wilson." This was followed by a laugh. "I mustn't let myself be amused just yet," went on the voice. "That can come when I see him a beggar in the street."

"So that's what you want?" said the Mayor, playing for time.

"That's what I've got to have. Listen, shorty, I'm sick of this talk. You want to stop murder? Break Wilson. Disgrace him. I'm not asking you this. I'm telling you. Get that, you fat guy." The words came pouring out. "I'll kill a girl a day until you obey me. They'll be your murders as well as mine. Well, how about it?"

"What's that? What's that you say? If I don't do it — if I let him stay in the department I am to be responsible for the death of more girls? It will be my fault as well as his? My friend, I'll tell you what I'll do for you." At this point the Mayor's voice was terrible. "I'll make it a point to come to your electrocution," and without realizing it the Mayor snapped the phone back on its cradle.

Doyle came hurrying into the office triumphant. "I think we've got him. He was phoning from a pay station at 125th Street and Third Avenue. I caught one of our cruising cars within five blocks of it. It's racing there now. And if that isn't luck, what is it?"

Then he stopped and stared at Wilson. "What's the matter with you?"

"I expect everything," said Wilson, "or nearly everything. You haven't got your man, I'm afraid."

"All right, boys," said the Mayor, "it's my fault. I lost my temper. I told him what pleasure I would take in going to his electrocution. I expect he got out of there in a hurry. I guess I've upset your applecart for you and I'm as sorry as hell."

"What was he like? Did you get anything from what he said?" asked Doyle.

"Wilson's right about that guy! He's nuts. I suppose, as Mayor of this great city, I should have said that I think he was deranged. But between us three we have a maniac on our hands. He offered to trade. He said if I got Wilson out of the department for disgraceful reasons he would stop the killings."

"I heard him," said Wilson. "He offered to make a trade. The lives of the young girls he is planning to destroy, for me. He didn't want to kill me."

"No," said Doyle, "he does not want to kill you. But what he does want is to destroy the career you have taken all your life to build up. He wants to rob you of the regard and friendship of many men and women who have come to you because you're a square guy. For some grievance, he has made up his mind that you have to go."

There was quite a long pause, and Wilson started to take a cigar out of his pocket but instead took the one the Mayor handed him and lit it. Then he spoke very slowly:

"What the man asks is a very simple matter. The life of any man over fifty has darned little value in comparison with that of a young girl. How can you tell what she would mean to life? Nor what life would mean to her. Suppose someone had killed Nancy Hanks — I mean before her marriage — so that there was no Lincoln. Destroy a girl and you don't know what you're destroying. You don't know at all. What can I do from now on? In ten years I'll be retiring. A middle-aged cop with flat feet and a pension. And the worst of it all is that I'll be glad to get the pension. So any time you like, sir, here I am, kick me out. Right now if you like. You can prefer charges against me — neglect of duty. And, your Honor, I'll go out with a light heart."

"You'll do that over my dead body," said Doyle. "Now, come on, fellow. Pull yourself together. You're no milksop. Someone calls up over the phone and threatens to kill a girl if you don't get kicked out of the police department, and you want to quit. That's not like you. I've seen you tackle gangs and strikers, political graft and a thousand and one things that have made this police department so hard to build up. Well, it's my department too. I'm the Commissioner. And I'm not going to get out and I'm not going to let any maniac run the police for me either. Of course if his Honor wants us out that's a different thing. He has the right to say, it's up to him. But his saying it won't make it just, and much as I respect you, sir, and admire you, I'll fight you on this. I won't let you destroy the department I built up, and Wilson stays.''

The Mayor rushed over to Doyle. ''Who do you think is running this? I'm the Mayor of this city. Bet your life Wilson stays. I'd be a fine guy to go home tonight and say a voice on the phone runs this city. Wilson, I want you to tell me one thing, and that very frankly. Will other girls be killed?''

''I'm practically sure of that, but because of that I'm practically sure I'll get the killer.''

CHAPTER 3

IF CAPTAIN WILSON had been on duty at nine o'clock in the evening at Pennsylvania Station, he would have seen an exceedingly pretty girl hurrying from a train. She had a funny little hat tipped over on one ear. Her blue eyes and dark hair were properly set off by a well-cut frock of a light blue. An alligator had worn her shoes in their original form and what had not been turned into shoes was used for her purse which was tucked under her arm. This was Mary Lester at twenty-two. She evaded a redcap with a smile and fairly ran through the station to the 33rd Street entrance. There, parked halfway down the block, was a taxicab. The driver was a well-built young fellow who, at the sight of Mary, made one step toward her and then stopped as if pulled back by an invisible hand. Then as she came up to the cab he opened the door and stood at attention with no sign of recognition beyond a slight nod. The girl said "Home, James," stepped into the cab, and they drove away.

Captain Wilson saw none of this but he did encounter the cab and the driver and the girl further uptown. Now the police often have intuitions, and these days and these nights Wilson's were sharpened almost beyond belief. And there was something about the careening of the car, something about the speed with which it was traveling that made him turn to his driver and order him to follow it. So he was less than fifty feet back of the car when it turned into a side street suddenly, then without warning stopped before a vacant lot. The lights were turned off, the driver sprang from the car, opened the door, stepped in, and the woman in the car screamed.

For four days Wilson had been cruising the streets hoping against hope that he would find some clue, some attempt at another murder. And here, by one of those wonderful chances, he saw a man suddenly jump into the cab he had been driving and Wilson heard a woman scream.

Wilson did not wait for his own car to stop; he jumped from it as it approached the other, threw open the door and reached in to prevent another murder.

"What the hell!" said the Captain, because the cab driver was kissing a very pretty girl and saying tenderly: "I'm so glad you're home, I'm so glad you're home." And then came a long and tender and very beautiful kiss. And at this point Captain Wilson's long arm shot out, grabbed the taxi driver by the shoulder and tried to pull him out of the cab. The girl screamed again. But this time it was another kind of a scream — a louder, shriller scream that employed the words: "Police! Help!" By this time Wilson had no difficulty in getting the taxi driver out of the car. The young man came out like a catapult with fists flying. At this point Lieutenant Evanhoe, who had been driving the Captain's car, stepped between the two men.

"What will I do with him, Captain?" he said.

The taxi driver himself interrupted at this point. "What

about me? What about this crook? So you're a cop, are you? I want to charge this chap with assault and battery. Tore my coat, yanking me out. Who the hell does he think he is?''

Evanhoe grinned at him. "He knows he is Captain Wilson of the Homicide Squad," he said.

Then the girl came out. "Officer, you got here very quickly after I called for you. It's wonderful. This man" — she pointed a dramatic finger at Wilson — "came into our car. I thought he was a burglar or something."

By this time Wilson had his breath back, his self-possession back, but his sense of humor was still missing. He turned to the girl. "I heard you call for help. I heard you scream."

Mary smiled at him sweetly. "You heard me scream," she said. "But I didn't need any help."

Wilson went on: "If more girls had screamed in time there would not have been three young girls murdered in this neighborhood in the last week. I'm in charge of the case. The whole show you put on looks funny to me. Cab tearing along, breaking all speed limits, turns into a side street, parks beside a vacant lot, guy jumps in and girl screams. Why shouldn't I think what I was thinking? If you've got any explanation for all this I'd like to hear it."

The taxi driver glared at him. "You're going to get it and you're going to get it quick and you're going to get it again down at headquarters. I'm no pushover for any cop that ever lived."

Evanhoe broke in: "Suppose you tell the Captain just what it all means. You were not trying to kill the girl, were you?"

Mary laughed. "Kill me? Perhaps with kisses. You wonder why I screamed, Captain? This is the man I'm going to marry. I've been away and this was our first kiss in over two weeks."

"Yes," said the taxi driver, "and if I haven't a right to kiss her, who has?"

Captain Wilson looked at them and grinned. "Listen, son, if she's your girl you got a right to kiss her. And if you can make her scream, more power to you."

"He can," said Mary Lester, "and he frequently does."

"But I've got to know more about you than the kissing," said the Captain. He turned to his lieutenant. "I think we'll take these people round to the station house for a minute."

"You don't mean we're being arrested?" said Mary.

"Not yet," said Wilson. "But I want to know a lot about you two people — a whole lot."

"Well, the way to find out about us," said Mary, "is to ask questions. Captain, why don't you get into the cab with me, and my boy-friend will drive us to the station, and you'll know where we are all the time."

"Wait a minute," said the taxi driver, "I don't know whether I like that idea or not."

Mary gave him a withering glance. "You'll do as you're told, my lad," she said; then, quite charmingly, in front of the two men, they kissed each other and laughed.

Then the Captain followed her into the cab and they drove away, with Evanhoe following.

At the station house the Captain led the way to the private office, followed by the girl and Raymond Watson, the taxi driver. Evanhoe followed them, and shut the door, and stood leaning with his back against it. The Captain pointed to a comfortable chair, and Mary dropped into it.

"May I smoke?" she asked.

"Yes," said the Captain with a sigh and lighted a cigar. "Anybody can smoke who wants to." Then his manners came back to him and he pulled out a box of cigars. "Have one?" he asked Watson.

Watson shook his head. Evanhoe pulled out a plug of chewing tobacco from his pocket and put it in his mouth.

"Now then," said Captain Wilson, looking at the boy, "who are you, what are you, and where are you from?"

"I come from upstate," said Raymond, "and I'm just through a medical course here at the College of Physicians and Surgeons. I'm on my own at last."

"Why the cab?" asked Wilson.

"Well, Captain," said the boy, "I had a good car and I had

no use for it. But I had a lot of ambition and no way of grati-
fying it. So I put my ambition and my good car together and
we turned it into a taxicab which I run at night as an inde-
pendent driver. I've been doing it for two years and I've
made enough to pay for my tuition at college and my ex-
penses.''

At this point Mary interrupted. ''Darling, that doesn't tell
the Captain very much, does it? I expect he wants to know
about tonight. You see, Captain, we're going to be married
tomorrow or the next day or shortly after that, and I had been
home to tell my mother and father about it and say goodbye,
because once you're married to a doctor you're kind of tied
down, you know.''

There was a short pause, then the Captain said, as if the
answer did not matter at all: ''Did either of you ever know
a girl named Maggie Cort?''

''Maggie Cort?'' said Mary. ''No. No, I don't think so.
Did you, dear?''

''No,'' said Watson. ''I've never heard of her.''

''Or a girl named Sarah Drake?'' went on the Captain.

''I'll have to make the same answer to that one,'' said Watson. ''I've never heard of her.''

''Or Caroline Hazzard? She was kind of a pathetic little
thing. A hunchback.''

''No,'' said Watson.

Then the Captain turned toward the girl. ''How about you?
Do those names mean anything to you?''

''No,'' said Mary. ''They don't.''

''You're sure about that,'' said Wilson.

''Why yes,'' said Mary, ''I'm sure. Should I have known
about them?''

''That's what we're trying to find out,'' said Captain Wilson. ''These three girls were murdered in this neighborhood
within the last ten days or two weeks. All of them were young
girls. And even the little hunchback was pretty. You're sure
neither of you have heard of them at all?''

The young people nodded.

"Well," said the Captain, "that's that. They were all killed in the same way — stabbed in the heart. But here is what I can't understand about it. There hasn't been any bleeding from these wounds. You're a doctor, I wonder if you could explain that to me?"

"Wait a minute," said Watson. "Let me think that over. Each one was stabbed in the heart?"

"Yes."

"Not one of them bled at all?"

"Not externally."

"And you want me to tell you how this was done?"

"Yes, if you can."

"What did the Medical Examiner say?"

"He's an old fogey," replied the Captain. "He said one thing or another. His principal explanation was that the knife had cut the heart so that it couldn't function, so there was nothing to pump blood. That was his theory."

"You couldn't call that a theory exactly," said Watson. "It seems to me —" and he leaned forward suddenly and picked up a paper-knife from the desk then walked over toward the girl.

"Now, suppose," he went on, "I wanted to kill Mary, and there was nobody around, and I wanted no blood, exactly as you describe it. I'd take the knife, jab it into the heart, then I'd move my wrist backward and forward very quickly. That would make the blade move back and forth four or five inches each time. There wouldn't be any heart left and there wouldn't be any bleeding. I'm not trying to tell you this in scientific terms, Captain. But that's how it could be done; I don't know how it was done."

"I see," said the Captain. Then after a pause he came closer to the young people.

"Did you read anything about these girls in the papers?" he asked.

"No, I didn't," said Mary.

"How did that happen?" asked the Captain.

"All I've been reading in the papers has been the women's

pages. I wanted to buy a trousseau for about ten dollars, and that takes a lot of studying.''

The Captain laughed. ''I've got a daughter of my own. I know. Now there is just one more thing I'd like you to do, and that is to go with Lieutenant Evanhoe and leave your fingerprints here — just for the record.''

''Then,'' said Mary, ''we're not under arrest?''

''No,'' said the Captain, ''not yet, anyway.''

CHAPTER 4

MARTHA WILSON LOOKED at her mother and laughed. ''There are two things,'' she said, ''that I want to know about. You never tell me, you're always making excuses, but I hope that some day you'll realize I'm a grown woman and will let me into the secret.''

Mrs. Wilson looked at her daughter. These two were always laughing at each other.

''All right,'' said Mrs. Wilson, ''I'll tell.''

The girl almost crowed. ''I knew that eventually I'd break you down. First I want to know why you prepare a hot foot-bath for Father every night at six o'clock. He never uses it, he's never spoken about it. When he comes in you act as though you were ashamed of it. What's the secret?''

For a woman well over forty, Mrs. Wilson achieved a very effective giggle. ''Your father hasn't always been a police captain,'' she said. ''When we were first married we lived more simply than we do now, your father walked the streets hour after hour in shoes that were not very scientifically made. So I started our life together by giving him a hot foot-bath the minute he got home. Sometimes he would take off his socks and shoes himself, but I did it most of the time. For the first year or two I was a skinny little thing, and he'd put his feet in the tub and draw me up into his lap and there we'd sit for half an hour, warm and cozy and sweet. It got to be kind of a habit with us.''

Martha leaned over and kissed her mother. ''You couldn't sit in his lap now, darling.''

''I could so. It would be crowded, but the point is that some night he's coming home and he's going to look round for that bath and it'll be waiting for him. There's no secret about it. That's all; I'm just fixing something I know one of these days your father will want.''

''How long has it been since he used a bath like that?''

''I wouldn't remember. It's a good many years.''

''Ten?'' asked Martha.

''Oh, I think more than that,'' said her mother.

''Well,'' said Martha, ''I've heard a lot of things about marriage, things a woman should do to hold her husband. But I don't think anybody ever told me about washing his feet.''

''It's *not* washing his feet,'' said her mother indignantly. ''It's bringing rest to what is tired in him. Some day, child, you'll have a man of your own and you'll understand what it means. There'll be a hundred things you'll want to talk to him about. But when he comes home, there is one thing he wants — rest and quiet. And if you're a wise girl, that is just what you'll give him. And that will be just the same as a hot foot-bath. Now what is the other one?'' asked Mrs. Wilson, and at that moment the clock in the next room struck six.

''The other thing,'' said Martha, ''is that darn clock. It's the ugliest thing I ever saw.''

''It was a wedding present,'' said Mrs. Wilson. ''It's in the shape of a building in Rome or Athens or somewhere. I can't remember the name —''

''The name of the building,'' said Martha, ''is the Parthenon. But your clock is all black marble and brass. Why do you keep it?''

''Well,'' said Mrs. Wilson, ''there isn't much of a secret about that. It was a wedding present from a young fellow that I pretty near married. We honestly thought we were going to get married, and then your father came along. Maybe it was his uniform, I don't know, but I never could see anyone else after I saw him. So this young fellow sent me the clock. And he said a funny thing, he said when he brought it to me himself: 'I want you to keep it and hear it strike and I want you to know how much faster life would have gone had you been with me.' As if any happy woman wants life to go fast. There's your father now,'' she added.

That was another mystery Martha had never been able to fathom, how her mother knew when her father was about to put his key into the door. But it was Captain Wilson and the sag in his walk as he came into the room and the droop to the shoulders that usually stood out so square told his wife that the time had come again for the hot foot-bath.

''Well,'' said Captain Wilson grimly, ''what a day this has been!''

''Don't talk,'' said his wife. ''Sit here.'' Martha took her father's hat. Now Mrs. Wilson was on her knees in front of her husband. Quietly she unlaced his shoes, removed them tenderly from his aching feet, pulled off his socks. ''Oh, your poor feet!'' she said and said it happily.

Then, almost before they knew it, she had set the foot-bath down in front of him, and for the first time in nearly twenty years her husband was resting his tired, inflamed feet in a bath she had prepared for him. For a moment no one spoke.

''My God,'' said the Captain, ''that feels good.''

''That's right, dearie,'' said his wife, ''wiggle your toes.''

Wilson grinned at her and then turned to his daughter standing near. ''Now that's a funny thing about your mother,'' he said. ''How would she know to have that ready for me tonight of all nights? I'm home to dinner every night at this time and there's never any talk about a hot foot-bath for me. But every step of the way home tonight I was saying to myself, 'There was a time she'd have a hot foot-bath ready for me if my feet were blazing like a pair of bonfires.' And here I drag my tired dogs into the room and, by golly, here is the bath all ready for them. Now that's what I call intuition.''

Both women laughed. ''What have I said that's funny?''

asked the Captain. His daughter leaned over and rumpled his hair and kissed him.

"You wouldn't understand at all, Father. It's just a secret between me and Molly."

Wilson tweaked the end of his daughter's nose. "The more secrets you and Molly have together, the better it'll be for you and the better it will be for the man you marry. The secrets that woman can tell you. . . ."

Mrs. Wilson looked self-conscious. Martha was in her element. She had a chance to tease her father and mother at the same time. "Father," she said, "do you honestly think Mother knows more about married life than most women?"

"That," said the Captain, "depends entirely on what you think marriage is for. To take a guy like me who's not worth much and make a man out of him, and a happy man of him all these years, I'd say your mother knows more about marriage than any other woman in the world. Think of it, all the years we've been married and there hasn't been hardlly a time when I've wanted to bat her over the head. In fact, not once, now I look back at it. And that's a record for a red-headed guy like me. And here we are, all three of us, happy together. Our home is not very big but it's big enough for us. We don't have roast quail every night but do you smell that corned beef and cabbage out there waiting for me?"

And then the telephone bell rang.

"I'll take it," said Martha as she started toward the phone.

"Never mind," said her father, "it's for me."

"You'll sit there and rest your feet," said his wife.

So after all it was Martha who got the news.

She turned very white as she listened to the message as it came over the phone, then finally she said: "Yes, I'll tell him right away," and put down the receiver.

After a pause she said: "The Commissioner wants you downtown right away, Father. He said you'd better not wait for your dinner."

And instantly all the fun went out of the lives of these three.

"What did he tell you, daughter?" asked the Captain.

"Nothing, Father. He said you'd understand, case number four."

And now Wilson stepped into his shoes and his wife was lacing them hurriedly. She had not spoken. She had not looked at him. She was all duty, all work. Then they kissed and Captain Wilson went downtown.

Commissioner Doyle was chewing his cigar and tramping back and forth across his office when Wilson arrived. Wilson yanked off his hat, hurled it at a settee on the other side of the room, lit a heavy cigar, and sat down. There was a short pause. "All right," he said, "I'm here."

"This time," the Commissioner said, "he got a bride of a year, and to get that cold knife of his into her heart quickly he had to jab it through the baby she was holding to her breast. A month-old child and its mother."

"No other details?" asked the Captain. He was white and shaken.

"Yes," said the Commissioner, "there are two other details. It was the same neighborhood, but just to make it pleasanter for us, the latest victim lived with her husband and her baby almost across the street from the station house. I'm beginning to wonder—" went on the Commissioner.

"It's about time. All around there, all alike. What's the other detail?"

The Commissioner picked up a sheet of paper from his desk and handed it to the Captain. This is what it said:

"I sent you one warning. Why don't you pay attention to me. This is the last warning. I'm going to kill a girl every day that Wilson stays in the department. Do you want to keep him? That's the price you've got to pay. I have shown you how easy I can do it, and I am smarter than your whole darn police department. I want Wilson thrown out. I'll promise you this, Commissioner: Wilson goes or there is a murder a day. And by the way, I'm tired of this neighborhood and I think

I'll move. Greenwood Square is nice and quiet, isn't it?''

Very quietly Wilson put the paper back on the Commissioner's desk, and the two old friends stared at each other.

The Commissioner said: ''Done exactly like the other letter, you see. And no prints again.''

''Of course that's the finish,'' said Wilson. ''I can't have these deaths on my conscience. Kick me out. I've had enough. I can take a certain amount of punishment, but four is plenty. I've had enough.''

The Commissioner jumped to his feet quickly and stood staring at him. ''No, by God,'' he said. ''You haven't had enough. And I haven't had enough. Do you know what makes the police valuable? It's the courage and fidelity of the men who are in it. We've got thousands of men—a small army of them—and they, all of them, face death when they have to. I guess they know there isn't one of us who wouldn't do the same thing. Now, then, Captain Wilson, what were you going to say to me?''

''Just this. I'll stick as long as you want me to, but when you've had a bellyful of this, sing out and throw me to the fish. Only, if I stick, all the rules are out. I'm going after that fiend and I'm going to get him but I'm going to get him in my own way.''

There is a certain amount of formality about entering the office of the Police Commissioner in New York. Just outside the door there is always a policeman on guard and before you come to him you pass another guard at the door which opens into the outer office. But there is one man in New York who pays no attention to these guards or to announcements; he comes and goes at will. Not only at Police Headquarters but in any other municipal building. And when he came into Doyle's office on this occasion his face was white. He did not take off his hat. He did not drop his cane or his gloves. He just stood inside the door and glared at the two men.

''Well, Mr. Mayor,'' said the Commissioner, ''I see you've heard about it.''

''I've seen it. I've just come from the place. I told them not to touch either of the bodies, Wilson. I want you to go up and take a look at them yourself. A mother of twenty who looks about sixteen, covered with the blood of her own dead child. And no clue. I'm getting sick of that phrase, boys. No clue. Don't you think it is about time someone connected with this department did a little work?''

"Yes," said Wilson, "I do."

Suddenly the Mayor's manner changed. He walked over to the Commissioner and reached into Doyle's pocket and took out a cigar, which he lighted. Then he sat down. After a pause he said: "We're in a hell of a mess, aren't we?"

"Yes," said Doyle, "we are."

"We are and we're not," said Wilson. Then, leaning over, he picked up the second letter from the murderer and handed it to the Mayor.

No one spoke while the Mayor read. Then he leaned forward and put it very quietly on the desk. "The man's crazy," he said. "I knew that when he phoned."

Captain Wilson said: "But, crazy or not, he's killing young girls, and he says he'll stop it if I get out of the department—if I'm kicked out of the department. My first feeling was that I would get out. To hell with him. Then another thought came to me. We've got something in this department of twenty thousand men that they call morale. It is very precious. It's a thing that takes a long time to build, and it's a tough job to rebuild it when it's broken. Your kicking me out of the department or my sneaking out of it in this case wouldn't do that morale any good. So I'm going to get that guy."

"How?" asked the Mayor. "That's the talk. You've got a plan?"

"I have. We all think this guy is a nut. Let's assume he is crazy enough to do exactly what he seems to say he'll do— move to Greenwood Square for his next crime. It's the only assumption we can make. And since he's just killed his fourth young girl and her child, we are fairly safe in thinking he won't kill again for twenty-four hours. Let's send our men in there tonight and have them go through that precinct with a fine-tooth comb. I'll have the name, address and identity of every man, woman and child in it. The location of every lodging house and the number of vacant rooms available at this time in each one of them. I want to know about the stores in the district. I'll want twenty men from the detective bureau to do this work.''

''You'll have them,'' said Commissioner Doyle.

''All right. Then I'll want you to announce that this is my last chance. Say that while you've got faith in me, and I've been a good cop, you feel that if there are any more murders of this kind—I'll have to go, I'll be kicked out of the department.''

''I wouldn't let that happen,'' said Doyle.

''All right, but you could say it was going to happen, couldn't you? We don't know anything yet. We've had two crazy letters. We've heard a crazy man threatening on the phone. These messages may have come from some crank that had nothing to do with the murders at all. But if you make this announcement about me and then murders of this kind start in Greenwood Square where he said he might go—'' He leaned forward suddenly and picked up the second letter. ''Come on,'' he said, ''let's get at it.''

CHAPTER 5

POLICE COMMISSIONER DOYLE SPOKE his little piece and it went something like this: ''Captain Wilson has been a hard-working and thoroughly honest policeman for over twenty-five years and we can't ignore that record. At the same time, these murders must be stopped. The Mayor is emphatic about that, and they will be stopped. We have given Captain Wilson a week in which to solve these murders and arrest the killer. If he doesn't succeed, he'll have to get out.''

This speech as it appeared in print didn't sound in the least rehearsed, but it had been thought out and written out. And when Wilson went to Greenwood Square the next day he carried under his arm a briefcase containing a complete census of the square. Every man, woman and child, every apartment house, every store, every rented room and every room that was to be rented. He had a special staff, men who had worked with him for years. Evanhoe and Vallely, his trusted right and left hands, were among them.

And so the lines of battle were drawn.

Greenwood Square lies in a very old part of the city. The houses in Greenwood Square were old, the rooms had high ceilings and the halls were wide. They were something like the ancient houses in Washington Square. Some of them were lodging houses. Some had converted their lower floors into stores. There was the inevitable bar.

Greenwood Square was far enough away from main thoroughfares to be quiet. The rumble of traffic came to it remotely. Some of the people who lived in these houses recalled that their grandmothers or grandfathers had first built them. Others had rented because they thought the district was quaint, which it was. But the last thing the square looked like was a trap set to catch a murderer. The police investigation about the occupants of the houses and the stores of this district had been carried on so circumspectly that it had aroused no suspicion at all.

Here was a district that knew policemen only vaguely. Occasionally one would drift in and give it the once-over. It was a quiet, steady district.

Monahan, who owned many of the houses and acted as renting agent for the others, slept for hours on warm days in front of his real estate office in one of the buildings. As he used to say with a gurgle of laughter, Greenwood Square was part of Philadelphia which had been mislaid and dropped into New York in some mysterious manner. That was his pet joke.

At ten o'clock of an August morning in 1941, Captain Wilson walked into the station house of the 41st Precinct and opened his fight for the capture of the killer. And about the same hour James Hooper, a tall, saturnine-looking man of about thirty-five, walked briskly into Greenwood Square. He carried a heavy handbag on his left shoulder and a suitcase in his right hand. Back of him came a man with a pushcart loaded with baggage. At this hour of the morning the square was fairly crowded. Children were running about playing. James Monahan was seated out in front of his little office, half-asleep and drowsily hoping against hope that no business would interfere with him. Hooper came to a stop in front of him and stood looking at him with a wide grin. He coughed once and then Monahan awoke.

"Oh, hello," said the real estate dealer, "so you're back."

"Yes," said Hooper, "I'm back and I'm taking that flat you showed me yesterday. It's the best I've seen."

Monahan grinned. "This side of Park Avenue anyhow."

Hooper lit a cigarette and laughed with him. "I mean for the money," he said.

"So did I," said Monahan. "Well, the door is open. That's the kind of a neighborhood this is. You'll find all the keys on the table in the kitchen. There's a grocery store round the corner and the nearest bar is that place over the other side of the square. Over on Seventh Avenue, next to the grocery store, is a Chinese laundry. Next to that is a butcher's shop. And while there ain't no connection between them, there's an undertaker in the same block. Colossal Pictures is on Seventh Avenue, and Super-Gigantic Pictures is right across the street. You going to pay your rent today?"

"Yes," said Hooper, "right now."

"Any time at all will do," said Monahan, holding out his hand. Hooper paid his rent and, turning to his baggage carrier, showed him the way up a flight of stairs to the flat he had just rented.

At that particular moment a shade in a front window of a house almost next door went up with a bang and disclosed, sitting in a big chair at the window, a fat, smiling woman of about fifty. The window sill had been widened and upholstered and on it reposed a glass and a pitcher, some cigarettes, and a couple of books. Mrs. Durkin, the tenant, was a helpless cripple, and all her waking hours were spent propped up at this open window.

For ten years Mrs. Durkin had heard every whisper that crossed the square. She enjoyed all the scandals, she shared all the joys of her neighbors, and it would only be fair to admit that she shared, too, all their sorrows. A woman with a quick tongue and her own peculiar sense of humor.

With the clattering of Mrs. Durkin's window shade, the quiet square seemed to take on a new life. Her high-pitched voice rang out gaily. First she called across the street to the bar: "Hi, Mike!" Mike, the bartender, appeared in the door-way for a minute and waved to her. "Cigarette me," shouted Mrs. Durkin.

"Right away, lady, right away."

This was their daily practice. The minute Mike heard her voice he knew what Mrs. Durkin wanted; he ran back into the bar, grabbed a package of cigarettes, trotted quickly over to her window and tossed them up to her. With a greedy hand Mrs. Durkin reached out and caught them. Then she leaned forward and called to Monahan. At her shout Monahan wad-dled out of his office and came toward her window.

"What's that new fellow's name?" she called, and before Monahan could answer, the newcomer was leaning out of his window. He looked across at Mrs. Durkin and laughed.

"The name is Jimmy Hooper, ma'am. Glad to know you."

Mrs. Durkin grinned. Then as she lit a cigarette she called back at him: "You're a good-looking devil, aren't you? Come up and see me sometime."

"All right, Mae. I'll do that."

And so Greenwood Square was getting into its stride for the day. Women came out of their homes through basement doors with market baskets. Little children, half-naked because the day promised to be a scorcher, played, ran and screamed and had a wonderful time. Monahan turned back into his office and called up the police station and left word that a new tenant had moved into one of his flats and gave a description of him. Collins Nash, a resident of the square, long out of work and not looking for it, came out of the bar and stood talking to the bartender.

"Kind of a nice day, ain't it?" said the bartender.

"Yes," said Nash. "Swell. Of course this is not what we'd call nice weather out in L.A. But you can't get weather like that back East here. By the way, what were all the cops doing around here last night? Anything to do with all these murders that are going on, do you suppose?"

"I don't know," said the bartender. "Funny thing, those cases."

Impinging on this conversation and high above the noise of the square was the sound of a violin being played very well. It was Hooper, the new tenant, who came and stood in the window with a violin tucked under his chin. He stood there playing and looking out on the crowd and smiling.

"Good, ain't it?" said the bartender.

"Yes," said Nash. "Wonderful. God, how I hate music."

A few doors away Minnie Schultz lived in her little house. Minnie was nineteen, with no job and a vaulting ambition as to silk stockings and such. She had, as she often said herself, "no gift for work." This morning she was ready for almost anything. She had done a good job with her hair, and she looked trim and clean. She brightened perceptibly as she heard the music and saw the new man. Who knows, who could tell what might come of that. . . . Then she called: "Goldie."

Goldie answered from an adjacent house: "I won't be a minute."

Then Minnie Schultz called, "Well hurry up, Goldie, I'm nearly dressed." And to prove that she was, Minnie came running out of the house. She threw a searching and fleeting glance at Hooper as he stood at the window. As Hooper looked at her he said to himself: "I wonder." And as Minnie turned away from him after her one glance her little bird brain said: "I wonder." She stopped for a minute under Mrs. Durkin's

window and laughed and chatted with her, and then swished
her way across the square to the front steps of the bar, where
she stood talking to Nash and Joe the bartender.

It happened—and there's no sense in laboring the how and
why of such happenings—that Mary Lester and her young
taxidriver-doctor fiance, Raymond Watson, were living in little Greenwood Square, he in one apartment, she in another.
Mary, hurrying in from a case with her suitcase, in which were
her nurse's uniforms, looked up at the window of Watson's
apartment. Old Mrs. Durkin saw her and called out of her
window:

"He's not home yet, dearie. How did you get home so quick?
Your patient die?"

"No," said Mary, "she's getting well."

"I suppose that's because of your fine nursing."

"Well," said Mary, "there wasn't very much the matter
with her. She really didn't need a nurse at all. Hot, isn't it?"

Mrs. Durkin grinned at her. "For a girl that's about to be
married you look kind of cool. Scared?"

"No, I'm not scared. I'm happy and I'm excited and I'm
delighted. I wish you could come to the wedding."

"Is it going to be in a church with a minister and everything?"

"Oh yes."

"Going to have a big reception?"

Mary laughed. "We've taken Madison Square Garden."

"Mary," said the old woman after a pause, "what are you
going to do really? What are you going to wear? It's a funny
thing, but you wouldn't think I'd be interested in weddings
after all these years. But I am. They say I'm a vile-tongued
old hag, but I'm wishing you and that boy of yours all the
happiness in the world. I don't know any two people I'd rather
see get along. I watched you from the first time I saw you give
him the glad eye."

"I did nothing of the sort."

"Don't lie to me. I saw you. And that was three years ago.
That's a long time to wait, isn't it?"

"Yes," said Mary, "it's a long time to wait. But, Mrs. Durkin, there's a big difference between marrying a cab driver and a doctor."

"Same man, isn't it?" said Mrs. Durkin.

"I'm not so sure about that," said Mary. "Not a bit sure. Cab drivers have got one way of looking at life and doctors have another. And I think I like the doctor's point of view best."

"You going to keep on nursing after you're married?" asked Mrs. Durkin.

"Yes. Until I have something of my own to nurse. It seems pretty wonderful to me for a nurse and a doctor to be married. What could bring them closer together?"

Mrs. Durkin laughed. "I knew a girl once fixed just the way you are, Mary. Nurse marrying a doctor. And she came to me about it and said she was going to give up nursing. She was going to take up something that would bring her closer to her husband."

"Closer to her husband than nursing!" said Mary. "What?"

"Embalming," said Mrs. Durkin, lighting another cigarette and waving at Minnie Schultz.

Minnie had stopped on the steps of the bar. She grinned at Joe, patted young Nash on the cheek, and, nodding in the direction of Hooper and his violin, she asked: "How did he get here?"

"Just moved in," said Joe. "Kinda good-looking, ain't he?"

"Yes," said Minnie, "he's all right. Kinda thirsty weather, isn't it?"

"Yes," said Joe, "and I owe you and Goldie a drink. As soon as she gets down from that bath of hers—" At that moment Minnie did something few girls can do. She put two fingers between her lips and gave a shrill whistle. From Goldie Newmark's house came an equally shrill whistle.

"Goldie will be right here," said Minnie. "We don't have to sit out here in the sun all this time, do we?"

"No," said Joe, "we don't. How about you, Nash? Want another drink?"

"No, I don't believe I will. Doesn't do me any good and I don't believe I like it anyhow." As Nash walked away, Goldie, in a gay thin muslin dress, with sprigs of apple blossom on it making it even more Spring-like, erupted from her house and made a beeline for the bar.

Thus the tapestry of life was weaving in little Greenwood Square.

Young Watson arrived and caught Mary just as she was turning away from old lady Durkin. Gus Smith, the postman, limped through the alley which was the only way into the square or out of it. As he blew his whistle and was about to enter the first house, Watson called to him.

"With you in a minute," Smith said over his shoulder.

"Oh, come on over now and take it, can't you?" said Watson. "It's just a change of address."

Smith crossed the square. "Moving away from here?" he asked and reached into his pocket for a change-of-address card.

Mary giggled. "He won't need that. He's giving up his flat and coming to live with me, that's all. Name's the same, only he'll be at number 7 instead of number 4."

"For goodness' sake," said the postman.

"Don't be an ass, Smith," shouted Mrs. Durkin from above. "They're going to be married."

"Oh, I see," said the postman. "When's all this going to happen?"

"Tomorrow," said Mary.

"Well," said the postman, "good luck to you and a lot of children, if you want them. Some do." Then he went back to the first house.

Mrs. Durkin called after him: "Say, Smith, did you hear about all the cops we've been having around here?"

"No, I didn't. What difference does it make? The only difference between cops and postmen is that postmen's feet are flatter."

CHAPTER 6

NOW THIS WAS THE BIG DAY in Minnie Schultz's life. She had just about made up her mind: she wasn't going on as she had been living; as she said it to herself, she was "going to make a change."

Minnie was a pretty little thing—well built, blonde, with all the hot blood of an icicle. She had watched with envious eyes the getting of easy money.

This too was the day that Mary Lester and her young doctor were to be married, and it was thirty-six hours since the police had gone so carefully through all the houses on the square. Nothing had happened the first day. Captain Wilson had gone into the station house, talked to his men, wandered around the entire precinct. There had been no more murders. The arrival of a few cops had made little difference to the people who lived in the square. A quiet, uneventful neighborhood. A friendly neighborhood, full of gossip and talk of all kinds, mostly small.

Mrs. Durkin had just finished her lunch and with a lighted cigarette between her lips was leaning out of the window, her old face alert as she watched life weaving in and out under her amused eyes. Minnie, coming out of her house, gave a quick glance up at Hooper's window and smiled as she saw him.

In a moment Goldie joined Minnie. As the girls disappeared into the bar, Hooper, who had been standing at his window unseen, ran down the stairs and dashed into the street. Monahan called to him: "Hey!"

"Who? Me?" asked Hooper.

"Yup," said Monahan. "Is everything O.K.?"

"It will be," said Hooper, "as soon as I get a drink. Who are the dames?"

"Well," said Monahan, "one of them is a stenographer and the other ain't."

"Which is the one that ain't?" asked Hooper.

"The little blonde one," chuckled Monahan. "She moved in here when she was about six years old. She and me used to talk quite a lot. Sort of restless. Always looking for some fellow to suit her—I mean some fellow with money."

"I see," said Hooper, "that sounds kind of interesting. What do you suppose she calls money?"

"Oh well," said Monahan, "she always has been sort of ambitious."

There was no one in the bar but the two girls and the bartender. A great-hearted compassion had moved him and he had given the girls a drink, which they had just finished at a small table at the side. They were now talking about the pursuit of happiness, new hats, more drinks and what Goldie called life.

"Well, well," said Hooper as he entered the place. "A couple of schoolteachers. I bet you could teach me a lot of things."

"How about some manners," said Goldie.

"Oh, I know, I know," said Hooper. "Good afternoon, ladies. Isn't it a lovely morning? How about a drink?" Then he went on. "What's the matter with the off-twin? Not afraid of me, are you?"

Minnie giggled. "I guess I am, a little, perhaps."

"Aw, shucks, you mustn't be," said Hooper.

Minnie looked him over. Her glance took in his well-polished shoes and every item of his good clothes and rested approvingly on his scarf pin.

"Well, whatever you say," said Minnie finally.

"I say we have a drink," said Hooper. "I'm a stranger here myself. You see I've just moved in."

"I know that lonely feeling is terrible, isn't it?" said Minnie. "The world is so big and we're so little." She giggled. "I remember you now," she went on. "You're the gentleman who played that lovely hymn on the violin. It must be lovely to play a hymn."

"Yes," said Hooper, "it is. You must come up and see me

some time and I'll play it for you."

Goldie looked at him quietly. "That's a new one! Haven't you got any etchings? Could we take a rain check for the drinks? We just had one."

Hooper came closer to them and stood looking down at Minnie. There was a question in his eyes and an entirely blank look in hers. She had made up her mind to give nothing away, not even a glance. "Come up any time," went on Hooper. "Gee, but you're awfully cute. Come on up and we'll try a whisky and soda." And with a grin he walked away.

"My God," said Goldie, "but he's fresh!"

"His clothes look pretty good, don't they?" said Minnie. "Now I wonder. . . . Some of those musicians make quite a lot of money, don't they?"

"My goodness!" said Goldie.

"Well, it's got to be somebody," Minnie said, shrugging her shoulders. "Goldie, I'm gonna marry that guy if I can hook him.

"And why not?" she went on. "I haven't got the gift for work. Everybody says I'm dumb. No decent clothes. Ten-cent perfumery. I'm straight and darn near naked."

"I heard all that before," said Goldie. "And what about loving the man you marry?"

Said Minnie, "What's so wonderful about love and marriage? My mother was married. She loved her husband and he walked out on her. They let her get married and never told her a thing about what marriage was. Goldie, there's just one thing a girl should be told before she gets married. I know that much."

"Don't be old-fashioned," said Goldie.

"I don't mean that at all," said Minnie. "It's about hats. Nobody ever tells a bride about hiding her husband's hat. That's the most important thing to know about marriage. Keep your hand on your husband's hat. They don't seem to like to go out bareheaded. The day I was born Pop took one look at me, and there was his hat lying on the table. And of course he grabbed it. And out he went and hasn't stopped going yet. So what did love get my mother?''

Minnie started out of the bar with a rush. Goldie stopped her. "Listen, Minnie! Don't make a fool of yourself. Come back in and sit down and let's talk it over. Maybe you're right. Maybe you're wrong. How do I know? It's your business, sure. But I'm not going to let you throw yourself away on that bum who was in here kidding us. A musician, what's that? A guy that plays a fiddle for a living.''

"Oh, I don't know," said Minnie. "I hear some of them make a lot of money, a lot of money. And anyhow, Goldie, I wasn't thinking about him much.''

"You know I'm your friend, don't you?" said Goldie.

"Sure," said Minnie, "I'll talk it over with you. I don't want to be stubborn." So they sat down again and this time Goldie bought a drink and they talked some more.

So many things happen at once. As the girls started to talk about the pursuit of happiness there were two other people talking about it as they came into the square again.

Young Watson had a small sign under one arm and Mary Lester under the other. In his right hand he held nails and a hammer. They stopped and he nailed the sign on the wall by the side of the front door of the house. He was very proud of this sign. He had painted it himself, black with gold letters on it: "Dr. Raymond Watson—Up One Flight." He backed away from it. Mary squeezed his arm. "It's beautiful. Beautiful. And think what it means to us! Dr. Watson and wife beginning life. I'm so glad I'm a nurse because I can help you a lot, can't I?''

"Of course you can.''

"There's just one thing I wish," said Mary. "I wish you'd get rid of that taxi. Driving around at night. Haven't you enough to do?''

"Darling, you mustn't be sore on the old bus," said Watson. "It paid my way through college, it's given us the money to get married on.''

"Yes, I know, but everything's going to be different now. I'm giving up nursing so I can be home to keep house for you. But I don't want to stay home at night alone while you're driving around dressed like a taxi driver.''

''Oh, well,'' said the boy with a laugh. ''I might as well tell the truth. I'm selling the taxi.''

''Oh, darling!'' said Mary. ''And now, lambie, I've got to go. I won't be away long, just a few errands. I want more stockings for one thing, and other things that I didn't get.''

''Wait a minute,'' said the boy. She turned back toward him. ''I want you to be very careful when you—''

Mary laughed at him. ''I know. Be careful when I cross the street. And I mustn't get too tired. And it's not raining, of course, but I must not get my feet wet, I might catch cold. That's the trouble when a girl marries a doctor. She never knows when he looks deep into her eyes whether he is looking for love or liver.'' She kissed him suddenly and ran away toward the street.

As Raymond stood waving goodbye to the vanishing figure, Minnie and Goldie, arm in arm and looking for trouble, came out of the bar. The young doctor saw them, and turned away and started walking toward Monahan on the other side of the square. Minnie called to him. ''Ray!'' she cried.

He turned back and looked at the girls.

''Would you like to buy a couple of dying girls a few drinks?'' Minnie went on.

Watson grinned at her. ''Behave yourself, jail bait,'' he said.

''Would you for a kiss?'' asked Minnie.

''No,'' said Watson.

''Oh!'' said Minnie. ''You wouldn't give fifty cents for a kiss that long!'' She measured a distance of about a yard.

''Fifty cents for a kiss?'' repeated Watson.

''Yes,'' said Goldie with a grin. ''It's nice work, as the saying is.''

Minnie came closer to Watson, and put her hand on his arm. Then she said very quietly: ''Ray, will you lend me ten dollars? I'll pay you back soon.''

Watson stared at her. ''Ten dollars! Where would you get

ten dollars? Don't tell me you have a job!"

He put his hand in his pocket, then slowly withdrew it, empty. "Where's your money coming from?"

Goldie said: "She expects to string a fellow along. Thinks she can play with fire and not get burned."

"Oh no!" he said, "she won't do that."

Minnie lost her temper. "Who says I won't? You make me sick. I know how to take care of myself. And if I have to marry the guy, I'll do that, too. I was telling Goldie only a minute ago, I've never had a shampoo in my life, nor a facial, and not even a manicure. But them days are over. Now I'm going to have them all. And enough to eat and a few drinks. And I'll have a bath any time I want to. And I'm going to have solid silk underwear. Oh gee, I bet they feel grand. And I'm going to see all the movies I want to, and go places in the summer if I want to. Oh yeah, and I'm going to help my poor old mother too. But I've got to have the money, Ray."

Watson looked at her and laughed. "Talk sense, bird-brain. Of course you don't mean it."

Minnie came closer to him and put her hands on his shoulders. "Oh, come on, Ray, be a good guy."

Watson took her by the wrists and dragged her hands from his shoulders and gave her a little shake.

Mrs. Schultz interrupted this scene, but only for a moment. "Minnie," she called, "oh you, Minnie. I want you to come."

Minnie called back. "All right, all right." Then she turned to the others. "I won't have that to put up with either. Ordering me around."

Watson looked at her. "Minnie, I've known you ever since you were a kid and I wouldn't bother with you only—"

"What business is it of yours, or are you going to make it your business?" Minnie retorted.

"Look here, Minnie," he said, "I don't want to sound like a preacher, but I know what you're talking about, and you don't. There's nothing in it. Take it from me. Come down to the clinic with me some morning and see the girls who thought they could outsmart a man."

"I don't want to hear about that. You're just trying to scare me."

Then came the whining cry of old lady Schultz. "Minnie! Oh, Minnie!"

Without turning her head Minnie called back: "Well, what you want now?"

Mrs. Schultz knew just what she wanted. "On your way in you can go down the basement and get a jar of that jam your grandmother made us last summer. And I mean get it today, not next week."

"You see," said Minnie, "ordering me around like a child. You watch me, now. They'll be bringing me jam some day soon, and bringing it on a tray. And there'll be plenty of it."

"Yes," said Watson, "a poor little tramp."

Minnie screamed at him. "Don't you call me that name. Don't you call me that name," and she struck wildly at him.

"A tramp, that's what you'd be. I'd sooner see you dead."

Screaming with rage, Minnie slapped him again and again. Then she stopped suddenly and said almost in a whisper: "Dead. Dead like those other girls." She moved away from him screaming.

Watson, taking a step after her, called: "Minnie, Minnie, I didn't mean that exactly. I just wanted to explain to you."

Something in the way he said it, something in his look as she ran toward the house made her scream: "You keep away from me, you keep away from me."

Watson ran after her. "I didn't mean to hurt your feelings, I didn't mean—" And he followed her into the basement of her house.

CHAPTER 7

MRS. DURKIN, FROM HER SEAT IN the window, had watched this little scene with a good deal of amusement. More drama, more love, more life. Why should the doctor bother about her? He has a lovely girl of his own and they're going to be married this afternoon. And the right kind of way too— two people married and loving each other. Durkin, behave yourself.''

''Then,'' as Mrs. Durkin told her cronies later, ''things began to happen. A tall, well set-up man of about fifty came hurrying into the square and looked around. You could see he'd been trained to take everything in with one look. What I call an observant eye he had. A lot of people might have been fooled by him, but not me. One look at his feet and I knew all. My God, I said to myself, that's a good-looking cop! I knew I was right because right back of him came another fellow about the same age, but in uniform. A lieutenant he was. A couple of fine-looking, upstanding men, worth the while of any woman.

''Now there's a secret in my life. I suppose it's because I've been here at this window so many years that my hearing has become so sharp. And not only that; I can read lips too. As far off as I can see, I can hear. There's very little around here that I don't hear, thank God! You can buy newspapers and you can skim through books, but you sit here from daylight to dusk and you see everything.

''Take Mary and that young doctor she's going to marry. They've known each other—oh a long time. She took one look at him the day he moved in here about eight years ago, she was just a kid then, but I'm betting a cigarette that her heart gave one little thump—well, it's nice to have it that way. But it's given up that bumping and thumping now. It beats firm and strong because that is the only man she could see. And as men go he's all right. It's a beautiful love story. Where was I?

''Oh yes, a cop had come in in plain clothes. Well, sir, he walked over to Monahan, who was sitting in front of his little store leaning back in his chair and sleeping so comfortable. You know Monahan's isn't so far away from me that I can't hear everything they say. So I'm as good as anybody else to report what happened there. Anyway, this fellow came along and put his foot on the rung of Monahan's chair and down it came and up woke Monahan. And no sooner had the old man woke up than he began his automatic spiel—I've-got-two-flats-one-furnished-one-unfurnished.

" 'I'm Captain Wilson,' said the man. 'I had that check-up made here the other night.' So you see how right I'd been. He was a captain.

"Monahan started to get up, and the Captain sort of waved him to rest himself. And Monahan said: 'Captain, sit down and rest your feet.' So the Captain sat down and the other fellow came up, the one in uniform.

" 'This,' began Captain Wilson, but Monahan interrupted him: 'Nobody has to introduce me to Vallely.' Then he went on: 'Of course I haven't seen him since the day before yesterday, but I've known him for years.'

" 'So have I,' said the Captain. 'What about this new man who's just moved in here? The fellow you phoned in about?'

"Well, it's a funny thing the way things work out, isn't it? There, almost under my window, was the Captain. And in the flat next to mine—separated by a brick wall, and that's about all—was this new fellow. A good-looking devil too if ever I saw one—tall, dark, flashing eyes. Why, his teeth were so good you'd have thought they were false. And just at that minute he walked over to the window with a violin under his chin, and he could play! He could play the heart right out of your body! That's what he could do. And as far as I'm concerned that was what he was doing, darn him. Got me all soft and mushy and sentimental. It's a funny thing how everything connected with those few minutes sort of clings to me.

"The Captain said: 'What about this fellow? What do you know about him? Where does he come from? What's his name?'

"And Monahan says: 'Well, his name is Hooper, and that's all I know about him. Come in here with his luggage and pays me a month's rent in advance.'

" 'Does he seem all right to you?' said Wilson.

" 'Sure,' said Monahan. 'Just like other folks. Just like other men—young men. Hadn't been here ten minutes before he starts on the make for one of our younger set.'

"Well, I notice that just about then this fellow Hooper, who'd been playing right along and looking at the sky, wan-ders away from the window so I couldn't see him any more. I guess he went back to sit down. Anyway, he went right on playing. Then I sort of looked around the square again and saw young Doc Watson was just going into his own place there. I whistled at him and kind of laughed and we shook hands. You know the way prizefighters do. He shook his hands and I shook mine and we grinned at each other.

"Then I heard a sort of ringing of bells and things, then in comes one of them pushcarts piled up with flowers. Now that's a sign of all kinds of things. Geraniums, lilies, and all sorts of flowers. Of all the flowers I see in them wagons, you know what I like best? It's those little English daisies. They're pretty and gay and sturdy. And you know what the doctor done? He walked over to this fellow and looking up at me said: 'You know I'm going to get married this afternoon, Mrs, Dur-kin, and I'm going to get you a posy.'

" 'Sure,' says I, 'get me one of them flats of English daisies.'

" 'That what you want?' says he.

" 'Yes, that's what I want.'

" 'No, I'm going to get you something I like and that I want you to have.' And he gets me a couple of pots of helio-trope. And he held them up and showed them to me. 'My golly,' says I, 'I'd forgotten there was such a thing. How sweet they smell! They're certainly going to make this place smell sweet.'

"And right at that minute there came the gosh-awfullest shrieks out of the Schultz house you ever heard. You never heard such a thing in your life. Let me give you the picture. There was the doctor right under my window, full of happi-ness. Next door the fellow was playing his violin, sweet and tender and nice. A few doors further on there was the Captain

talking to Monahan, laughing and joking and smoking a cigar.
And the sun was shining on the square and everybody was
having a good time, and then old lady Schultz lets out these
screams. You never heard such sounds coming out of a woman's throat! She come tearing out of the basement screaming: 'It's Minnie! Oh my God! It's Minnie!'

"Now, I don't expect you to believe this. Captain Wilson
was sitting comfortably in his chair when he heard that cry.
And, without seeming to get up, without any effort that I
could see, he jumped about fifteen feet. I know that in less
than a second he was standing beside Mrs. Schultz and all he
said was: 'Where?'

"She pointed to the basement of her house. And Monahan,
who's a kind-hearted guy, always trying to help people in
trouble, came over and took Mrs. Schultz by the arm and made
her sit down in his chair. And there she sat, a little old woman
crying and saying: 'Minnie, oh my God, Minnie! They got my
Minnie!'

"There was a sort of a pause, maybe about a minute, while
people were asking what was wrong, and running out of their
flats, and then Vallely comes running out of that place blowing his whistle.

"And the only thing I noticed was that he stood in the middle of that little alleyway—the only way you could get out of
the square. And I noticed that when a fellow tried to go out
toward Seventh Avenue, Vallely gave him just one look and
waved him back and said: 'Nobody goes out of here, nobody.'
Then he blows his whistle again. And, so help me, in no time
at all the place was filled with cops. Cops in uniform and cops
out of uniform. I never saw anything like it before in my life.
It looked as if they had been waiting for it. Just like in a play
when out of the ground all the demons start springing up, just
that quick. And Vallely didn't wait for any orders, but knew
just what to do. And he didn't give orders, he barked them.

" 'Nobody goes out of here,' he says, 'nobody. Doesn't
make any difference what excuse they make. Nobody goes out
of here without a pass from the Captain. Twenty of you fel-

lows had better get on the outside of this square. There's a guy named Tony who has his stand out there, and he can see the back of the whole place. Ask him if he saw anybody come out of any back door or down any fire escape during the last half-hour.'

"And twenty of those cops went away on the run. I tell you I never saw anything like it. They were like a pack of bloodhounds.

"Then out of the basement comes the Captain. He looked nine feet tall. And for a minute he didn't say anything. He just stood there and looked around, then the first thing he said was: 'Monahan.'

"Well, sir, I've known Monahan twenty years, and I've never seen him run that fast. The Captain had told him to hurry, but, by God, he was like a scared crab.

" 'Monahan, have you got a flat on the ground floor that is unoccupied?'

" 'I got a whole house that's empty,' says Monahan.

" 'I want it,' said the Captain. 'Now. I don't want any furniture in it at all, except one room on the ground floor with a kitchen table and some chairs. Get them and come back to me.'

" 'You betcha,' says Monahan, and away he went.

" 'Now then, Vallely,' says the Captain, 'I want one of the doctors from downtown — Mulrooney, the Medical Examiner himself, if you can get him. And you'd better tell the Comissioner we've got another case right here. Tell him it's another young girl, killed the same way and with the same weapon. Not fifty feet away from where I was standing, and that I've got the place bottled up. Nobody is going to get out. Ask him if he wouldn't like to come up and see me catch the murderer.'

" 'Oke,' said Vallely, and ran into Monahan's office.

"Now let me see what happened after that. It's all pretty clear because — well, when you see a thing like that you don't forget it right away.

"Doc Watson came running out. He came right over and tapped the Captain on the arm.

"The Captain didn't see him, so he turned sharp to look at

him. 'What the hell you doing around here?' says he.

" 'I live here,' says Doc. 'I've lived here for eight years. I'm the fellow you arrested the other day.'

" 'Yes, I know,' said the Captain. 'Know anything about this case?'

" 'Yes,' said the doctor, 'I do, a little. I was talking to Minnie Schultz about half an hour ago.'

" 'Where?' said the Captain.

" 'Over there on the steps and then down the basement,' said Doc. 'She went down there to get a jar of jam for her mother.'

" 'What were you talking to her about?' said the Captain.

" 'Oh, a lot of things,' said the doctor.

" 'Well, you can tell me about that later on. Did you kill her?'

" 'Of course I didn't.'

" 'Got any idea who did?'

" 'No,' says the doctor, 'I haven't. Nor why anybody should kill her. She was a little fool; she wasn't worth killing.'

" 'All right, that will be enough from you for now,' says the Captain.

"Then the music from next door got louder. Now that was a funny thing, wasn't it? And this fellow Hooper came to the window and stood looking at the crowd. And the Captain heard him and saw him and says: 'Stop that music, will you? I want to talk to you.'

" 'Well,' says Hooper, 'there's nothing to stop you.'

"And then there was quite a time when nobody said anything. The Captain put his hands in his pockets and stood looking at the windows, and everybody stood around. And then he made the funniest speech I ever heard. He said: 'My name is Captain Wilson of the police department. For the last four or five weeks somebody has been going around town killing young girls. And I've been trying to find him. And this time I guess I have. While I was sitting right here not half an hour ago, Minnie Schultz was killed. She is lying down there in the basement of her own house right now. Nobody has gone out of this square since Minnie was killed. See what I mean? I don't know who did it. I don't know who has been killing all these girls. But the fellow who killed Minnie Schultz is listening to me talking right now, and I would like to say that the easiest thing for him to do is to say: "I did it, and for God's sake get me out of here." But he won't do that. He's got away with four murders, all exactly alike. But I can promise him this fifth one is his last. Now, ladies and gentlemen, I want you to help me. I call on you in the name of the law. Nobody is going to leave this square or go about their business till I get this man. No use trying, either, because I've got cops all around here like a chain. Nobody can get out. And right over here I'm going to have an office and I want you to come down here and tell me what you know. Everybody here will be welcome. Everybody here will be treated the way they should be treated. And I don't care how long it's going to take me and my cops and photographers and everything. And, you and your families, nobody can go out and nobody can come in.'

"Well, I stood it as long as I could. It was a nice speech and I liked the way he talked and I liked the way the whole set-up was working. So all of a sudden I yelled out: 'Oh, Captain!' And he looked up and saw me for the first time.

"Then he says: 'What do you want?'

"I says: 'Captain, I'm a cripple, and from early in the morning till dark I sit at this window. Been doing it for ten years. And there's nothing in this square I don't see, not a thing.'

"'O. K.,' says the Captain, 'I'll be right up.' Then he turns to Vallely and says: 'Right here for you, Vallely. You know what I want. Nobody better.'

"Then, just as the Captain was coming into the house, Smith, our postman, stumps in.

"Now by this time the Captain was getting nervous and he says: 'Well, what do you want? Know anything about this case?'

"'No I don't,' said Smith, 'but I'm going to get hell if I don't deliver my letters. Will you phone down to Station E and tell them I'm kept here?'

"'Don't be a durned fool,' says the Captain. 'Nobody's keeping you here. Go on and deliver your mail.' Then he raised his voice and says: 'Oh, Vallely, don't detain the Postmaster General any, he has his work to do.'

"Then I hear the Captain coming up my stairs two steps at a time."

CHAPTER 8

POLICE ROUTINE IS POLICE ROUTINE, cut and dried, regulated, unswerving, but it brings results. Two men in white with a folding stretcher had pushed into the little square, nodded perfunctorily to the police on duty, and disappeared into the basement. Three minutes later all that was left of little Minnie Schultz was on its way to the autopsy room in Bellevue Hospital.

Before that, however, men from the Bureau of Identification had gone through the basement with a fine-tooth comb. They had examined every inch of the walls and woodwork for fingerprints. They had sprayed their white powder around the edges of doors and on door handles, anywhere hands might have rested. Along the window sills there had been plenty of prints and these had been photographed. The floor had been gone over, and the steps leading down into the cellar. Footprints had been found. These had been photographed, measured and indexed. And so, at last, the police had what the old-timers of the Homicide Squad used to call a picture. It mattered no longer how many people walked down into the cellar, how many fingerprints or footprints were left, the police had everything tabulated, indexed and ready for use.

And now Evanhoe was in the house that Captain Wilson had asked for. He stood in an empty room facing the square. The room was unfurnished except for a kitchen table and some half-dozen kitchen chairs. He was watching two electricians as they worked. Finally one of the men made a last connection and looked up. He pointed to an ordinary dial phone. "This," he said, "is the general phone. Get you anywhere. And this one goes to Headquarters. I can put in one connecting you with the station house if you want it."

"No," said Evanhoe, "this will be all right. Headquarters can connect me through to the station house if I want it. What about the dictaphone, where's that?"

The electrician pointed to a chandelier almost overhead. "There's one in there will do for most uses," he said. "Then I've got a microphone right under that knot-hole in the table there. That's stepped up pretty high and will pick up anything — almost a whisper. Certainly anything in an ordinary tone in any part of the room. They're both connected to earphones in the room overhead. Better test it, hadn't you? I got one of my men up there now with earphones on, so you can try it if you like."

Evanhoe grinned and walked away from the table about twenty feet. Then, with his back turned to the table, he said: "This is Lieutenant Evanhoe testing the mike. Stamp on the floor three times if you get the routine test." Then he walked about half a dozen steps away and in a low monotone said: "One, two, three, four, Mississippi, Mississippi." Then faster: "One, two, three, four . . . " After a pause the man overhead stamped three times.

"All right," said Evanhoe, "keep set for business. Can't tell how soon they'll come in here and start to talk."

The electrician started out, and the one who had spoken said: "Well, Lieutenant, you know where to get me if you want me."

"Yes," said Evanhoe, "I know. But I guess we're all set. As you go out in the hall send in the stenographer, will you?"

The men disappeared and almost before Evanhoe had time to turn round a fat, red-headed man appeared in the doorway with a pencil in one hand and a notebook in the other.

Evanhoe looked at him and laughed: "Well," he said, "if it isn't Sadie. Come on in and sit down, sweetheart."

The policeman waddled over and sat down and Evanhoe took up the phone connected with Headquarters. "Lieutenant Evanhoe reporting," he barked into the phone. "What you got for us?... All right, shoot it along, let's have it."

Turning toward his stenographer, Evanhoe repeated in a monotone the report that was coming to him over the phone. "Autopsy report on Minnie Schultz. Report of Dr. Waters, Assistant Medical Examiner. No bruises or marks on the body. Cause of death, incised wound through the heart, made by a long-bladed weapon, two-edged instrument. Width of weapon two inches; length of weapon, about four or five inches. Weapon was thrust through the heart, twisted sharply, cutting the heart to ribbons. Bleeding all internal. Instant death. Age of girl, about nineteen. Body undernourished. Case identical in every respect with those of Maggie Cort and the other girls. Thanks. ... Yes, I'll tell the Captain."

As Evanhoe hung up the phone, Captain Wilson came in rapidly, carrying a sheaf of notes and papers which he laid on the table.

Evanhoe said: "I've got the autopsy report here, Cap. You want the notes transcribed?"

"Yes, you might as well." Then, noticing the police stenographer, he said: "Why, how are you, Muldoon? Haven't seen you in years."

"I'm all right, Captain," said the stenographer. "Kind of a funny case, isn't it?"

"Yes," said Wilson. "Funny as hell. Let me have those notes as soon as you can."

As the man went out, Wilson turned toward Evanhoe. "Well," he said, "what about it?"

"Doc Waters says the case is identical with the others," said Evanhoe.

"Raped?" asked Wilson.

"No," said Evanhoe.

"I'm glad of that. I think we've got the man this time. There's nothing to show that he left the square, and the things that old woman told me — enough gossip to sink a ship. Some of it may be good."

From outside the room voices filtered in, one of them saying:

"Doesn't Captain Wilson know that an afternoon paper

comes out in the morning? What's he going to do about it?"

"Hell," said Wilson, "the press!"

Then a woman's high-pitched voice could be heard above the rest: "A young girl has been foully murdered and we women demand —"

Evanhoe said: "The lousy press."

As Captain Wilson opened the door he shouted over his shoulder to Evanhoe: "I'll want Monahan when I get rid of these bums."

Through the open door surged a crowd of reporters, camera men, and women journalists. Wilson greeted them smilingly. "Well, boys and girls, it didn't take you long. Come on in. Come on in."

And they came, like a torrent. There were eight or ten of them. Casey Harris, a man of about fifty, with a quiet manner and a benevolent sense of humor, led the crowd. In Park Row they said he had been born with his derby hat on the back of his head. Then there was Miss Tewkesbury, thin, skinny, fifty-five, a lady bloodhound if ever there was one. She had worked on many murder cases. Her reports on the Lindbergh case had rivaled even those of Adela Rogers St. John.

For a minute there was complete silence and Harris moved a little closer to Captain Wilson and said: "Well, Captain, what about it?"

Before Wilson could answer, the high-pitched, tremulous voice of Miss Tewkesbury came through: "Yes, Captain. This poor, little murdered child."

"She was nineteen, Miss Tewkesbury," said Wilson, "and she was five foot six in her stocking feet, and she wasn't what you'd call a —"

"Ah," said Miss Tewkesbury, "but still a child ... "

Before she could speak again Harris cut in on the conversation. "Captain, I hear you have this place all bottled up. Impossible for anyone to get out; how about that?"

Wilson replied a little bitterly: "That doesn't apply to you gentlemen of the press. You can go any time."

"I see," said Harris. "Do you want to tell us anything about this new murder that has again shocked the city?''

Then the questions came thick and fast, one on top of the other. Who was the girl? Any clues? Had she been attacked? Wilson laughed a little. ''Wait a minute, boys. One at a time. Don't rush us. This case is exactly like all the other ones. There's no difference at all. The girl was stabbed through the heart with a stiletto of some sort. No bleeding. No fingerprints that amount to anything. We've made no arrests and probably won't — for a few minutes anyway. The girl's name was Minnie Schultz and she was nineteen years old.''

Miss Tewkesbury interrupted: ''And beautiful, of course.''

''Well, as a matter of fact she is good-looking — was, I mean. Mother's name is Annie. The body was found in the cellar of her house, right next door here. The mother found her. That's all I can tell you now.'' Then he went on: ''Harris, you were on the other cases; it will save your time and theirs too if you explain the details to these gentlemen. There's no difference at all, none at all.''

''Oh, we know all about the other cases,'' said another reporter.

''That's good,'' said Wilson. ''Then suppose you tell us who did them?''

Harris cut in quickly. ''Captain,'' he said, ''would it break your heart to remind you that some of us work on evening papers? How long after the murder did you get here?''

''Oh,'' said Wilson, ''I thought you knew. I was here when it was committed.''

Harris gave a quick look at his wristwatch. ''Oh, my God, and it's late now. Keep quiet, you bums. Come on, Cap, will you give us —''

Wilson broke in: ''I thought you knew. I had been here a little while when the murder was discovered.''

''How long had she been dead? Don't guess, I want facts.''

''About five minutes.''

''What did you do then?'' snapped Harris.

''Why, I began my investigation and —''

Harris screamed at him: ''Think of my starving wife and

children, Captain. Talk fast, don't let me lose my job. In the name of God what did you do?''

''Well, no one has been allowed to leave the square since then.''

The other reporters started to talk. Harris quieted them. ''Cap, this is what I want to know. From the time of your arrival at this square until the murder had been discovered how many people left here?''

''None,'' replied Wilson.

''It can't be true. Nothing like that could happen! You mean the murderer is hidden somewhere in this square?''

''Yes.''

''And he can't get away?''

''He can't get away.''

Harris dashed out of the door, followed by all but Tewkesbury. She stood watching them with a grim smile on her seamed old face. ''Nice boys, aren't they, Captain? Not too bright, but still — I had a chat with the girl's mother. Terrible what time does to mothers.''

''You had no right to talk to her without my permission. You know that perfectly well, Miss Tewkesbury.''

''She didn't say anything that made sense. Not a thing.'' And with a little laugh she sidled out, passing Evanhoe who was accompanying Monahan into the room.

Wilson waved toward a chair and Monahan eased himself into it. He took a number of papers out of his pocket and put them on the table in front of the Captain.

''There,'' he said, ''is the whole kit and boodle of them.''

And all through these proceedings the music of a violin had been coming from Hooper's room.

''Darn that fiddler,'' said Monahan. ''He's been going on like that all day long. Why don't you arrest him?''

''That's the reason I don't arrest him,'' said Wilson. ''He's been playing like that all day. He was doing it when I came in and was still at it when the girl was found. Couldn't be playing music and be down in the cellar murdering her at the same time. Get that, don't you?''

"No, I suppose he couldn't," said Monahan slowly.

Wilson pointed to the papers on the table in front of him. "Just what are these, Monahan?"

"Well, you asked me for them. It's a list of everybody living on the square. All about them — at least all I know about them, ever since I been here. Hope it's what you want."

"Yes, that's what I want."

Wilson stopped for a minute and listened to the music. "That fellow plays darn well, doesn't he? Evanhoe, open the window a little more will you? That's better. I can hear it a lot better. Do you know anything about music, Monahan?"

"Only that I don't like it."

Wilson laughed at him. "It's pretty nice after you get used to it. I was brought up on it. Funny how those things will come into your life, isn't it? I was on a post once not very far from the Metropolitan Opera House. And I used to sneak in and listen to the operas. That was way back. Heard all the famous singers — Caruso, Emma Eames, all of them." He stopped and listened again. "Ah, here's where he gets it in the neck, through this passage. Fritz Kreisler can play that without a break." He laughed. "So can Spalding, but the rest of them! Now listen: hear him falter?"

The Captain sat with a grin on his face while the others listened. And the music went on fluently, smoothly, with no hesitation, no break, no fumbling. This brought the Captain to his feet with a shout. "There's something funny about this," he said. "Evanhoe, send Hooper to me right away. Tell him to bring his fiddle. And while he's out of his room — Evanhoe, have you got a fine tooth comb?"

"Sure," said Evanhoe.

"Use it."

"And don't you think I won't."

The Captain turned to Monahan. "Now, then, Monahan, I have to have more. A lot more. Who is Hooper? Where did he come from? What do you know about him? What's the set-up over there where he lives? I've got to have all that before he gets here."

"Well, there's nothing more than what I gave you on that paper, Captain. He came here two days ago and looked over the place. Tried to chisel me down on the rent — nobody's done that to me in years."

The Captain ran through the memorandum on Hooper.

"You say he has rented the entire second floor of No. 11. How many rooms is that?"

"Well, there was originally a full-sized front room, running along the entire front of the house and a bedroom at the back. Well, I split the back room down the middle. Gives him a small-ish bedroom, but a nice kitchen. I put in a table and a coupla chairs and I called it a dinette. They like that."

The music had suddenly stopped. Wilson knew what that meant and grinned.

Monahan continued: "There ain't a bathroom in this suite. But there's a companionate bathroom-toilet out in the hall. You know, one of those everyone in the house uses."

"How about a fire escape?"

"Yes," said Monahan, "there's one of them too. Right outside the bathroom window."

Wilson laughed. "So if a lady was taking a bath and there was a fire and —"

Monahan broke in: "Well, that would be just too bad, wouldn't it? But it was the best I could do."

"What I was getting at was this," said Wilson: "Could anybody step out of the bathroom on to the fire escape . . . then where would he go?"

"When you're on any fire escape," said Monahan, "there are two ways you can go, up or down. If you go down you'll drop into a sort of alleyway that runs around the place."

"Do you think the man with the fruit stand," continued Wilson, "could see anyone doing that?"

"Couldn't miss it," said Monahan.

"Then suppose he went up; where would he land?"

"On the roof, and he could run from one roof to the other pretty near around the square. Come out in any house he wanted to."

"I see. Don't you keep the scuttles on these houses closed?"

"No, I don't. Not since I was arrested by the fire department coupla years back for breaking one of their fire laws and I was fined fourteen dollars. They're open all night."

"Monahan," said Wilson, "tell me this. Could Hooper have gone up his fire escape to the roof, run over the roof to the Schultz place, gone down the steps there into the cellar, and then come back to his place again?"

"Yes, of course he could, but he didn't, because he was playing the violin all the time. Don't you remember?"

"Yes," said the Captain. "I remember. He was playing the violin all the time."

At that moment in walked Hooper, urbane, smiling, with the fiddle under one arm and the bow in his hand.

"Did you want to see me, Captain?" he said.

Now it was Wilson's turn to smile. "Yes," he said "I did want to see you, Mr. Hooper, and I want to congratulate you on the way you played. It's beautiful, beautiful."

Hooper almost blushed as he walked toward the Captain. "I'm glad you liked it," he said.

"I'm never going to forget it. I don't know when playing has given me such a thrill. Been playing long?"

"Oh yes, ever since I was a little kid."

"That accounts for it. Your fingering is marvelous, marvelous. That is what interested me so much. That's why I asked you to bring your violin down with you. Lovely tone, hasn't it? Doesn't happen to be a Strad, does it?"

"No. It's not that good."

The Captain laughed. "Monahan here doesn't like music. But we don't care about that. Go ahead and play that thing again. I'd like to hear it."

As Hooper picked up his violin, Wilson continued: "There are one or two questions I want to ask you, too, while you are here."

"I can understand that," said Hooper. "Why don't you ask them? I can play and listen and talk all at the same time. I'm not playing from notes."

By now he was playing. Not loudly but softly, tenderly, with a good deal of feeling, and as he played he talked, not nervous at all, smooth, relaxed:

"I'm a stranger here, of course. Naturally you want to know something about me—who I am, what I am. You're probably saying to yourself, maybe he killed that girl. Captain, I did not. I moved into this neighborhood because it was cheap. And I moved out of my old house because my neighbors did not like my playing so much. Any time you want I can give you the whole history of my life—where I was born and everything. But as for killing that girl—what for, in the name of God? I didn't know her. Never even saw her till a little while ago. Why, Captain, you know I wasn't out of my room. Playing all the time. You heard me playing, didn't you? Saw me playing when I came over to the window and looked out, and you looked at me. You remember that, don't you? I was playing all that time, just as I'm playing now."

"Yes," said the Captain, "I heard you. Go ahead. I hear what you're saying and what you're playing."

By this time the music had reached the passage to which the Captain had already drawn attention. Hooper faltered. He missed a note or two. He stopped and went back and tried it again. As he did so he said: "I was never out of my room till you ordered me to come here." And again the music faltered, and again he tried. Wilson never took his eyes from the man. He just watched.

As the bad spot was passed, Hooper continued talking: "I was never out of my room, I tell you, never—"

And then from the hallway came the sound of the same violin solo, faultlessly played.

The door was flung open and in the doorway stood Evanhoe holding in his hands a small victrola. The solo continued, smoothly, beautifully, as played for the record by Fritz Kreisler. Evanhoe walked in and put the victrola down on the table. "I found this up in his room, Captain," he said.

The Captain looked at Hooper who stood staring at his victrola.

The Captain said: "Evanhoe, take that victrola back to Hooper's room and start the record from the beginning. Then go out through the bathroom window and up the fire escape and on to the roof, then over to the Schultz roof and through the scuttle and down their stairs to the basement. You can take thirty seconds—no, take a minute. Time yourself. Then come back the way you went."

Evanhoe hurried from the room with the victrola in his hands.

The Captain turned to Hooper. "Sit down, young fellow, and rest a minute."

Hooper was white and shaking. "I swear to God—" he began.

"That's not going to do you any good at all," said the Captain.

He took out his watch and held it in his hand. "I'm counting the seconds, my boy; I'm counting the seconds."

CHAPTER 9

AS THE DOOR CLOSED ON EVANHOE no one spoke for a minute. Monahan settled himself more comfortably; his head fell forward, his chin rested on his chest, and he prepared for a short nap. Hooper stood like a trapped animal, leaning against the wall, his eyes fastened on the Captain, who sat looking at him and while still looking picked up the telephone connected with Police Headquarters.

"Let me speak to the Commissioner. Captain Wilson speaking, Commissioner. I didn't bother to report on that murder. I knew you'd get that quickly enough, but I've got a suspect standing in front of me right now, and I have a notion he's going to talk."

"You'd better get over that notion," interrupted Hooper.

Wilson's voice was silky as he spoke over the phone: "That

was the man talking then, Commissioner. Says he's not going
to talk. I think he will. . . . Inspector Hunt's back, you said?
That's wonderful. Flew back from London? Well, I certainly
will be glad to see that old chatterbox again . . . Oh, that's
wonderful . . . I certainly will be glad to see him. Yes, I'll
let you know what this fellow Hooper says . . .''

As Wilson dropped the phone into its cradle, Hooper
snarled at him: ''You're trying to frame me, are you?''

Wilson laughed at him: ''Hooper, you've been reading a
lot of cheap detective stories. I think you're a dirty murderer, and I'm going to prove it if I can. But if you're not,
I'll be the first to say so.''

And then Evanhoe opened the door and stood grinning in
the doorway. ''I made it!'' he said. ''From the time I started
that music I was down and back before the record was three-
quarters finished—time to get from Hooper's room to the
basement and kill the girl and get back and wash my hands,
all inside of two minutes.''

Wilson turned once more to Hooper. ''Now what have you
got to say?''

''Nothing,'' said Hooper.

Wilson nodded slightly in the direction of the sleeping Monahan. ''Better get him out, Evanhoe.''

With a slight shake, Monahan was awakened; a tug got him
on his feet and a push started him on his way home.

''See you a little later,'' said Wilson, as the landlord stag-
gered out of the room. Evanhoe followed him to the door and
spoke to the group of policemen standing in the doorway
waiting for orders.

''Captain Wilson doesn't want to be bothered for a little
while. No one must come in. No matter who calls.'' And Evanhoe not only shut the door but locked it. Then he went over
and stood by the Captain, who was standing with his feet well
apart and his hands hanging loosely at his sides staring at
Hooper.

Speaking very slowly and very clearly Wilson said: ''Ac-
cording to law, I have to warn you that you don't have to

answer any of my questions. You have a right to have a lawyer represent you at this or any other time. And by law I am
compelled to warn you that anything you say to me now may
be taken down in writing and used as evidence against you.''

There was a brief pause and Wilson's manner changed.
''What you got to say?''

Hooper looked at him and then he began: ''I can explain
about that phonograph.''

''That will be nice. We'll come to that by-and-by. Why did
you kill that girl?''

''I didn't.''

Evanhoe said: ''And all the other girls?''

''I didn't kill any girl, and if you say I did it's a lie.''

''What did you come to this neighborhood for?'' asked
Wilson. ''You wrote the Commissioner you were coming here,
that's why. But you won't get away with it.''

''What the hell are you talking about? Why would I write
the Commissioner? I told you what I came here for. I wanted
to get peace and quiet, where I could play my fiddle.''

Wilson's face by this time was not a foot away from Hooper's, which was now twitching with fear. Wilson's was like
a mask.

''Did you think you could get away with that alibi?''
shouted Wilson. ''Playing a fiddle, hey? Yes, you did. Left
that phonograph running, then you sneaked down for a murder. Why? That's what I want to know. You're caught; don't
you see you're caught. Why did you kill her?''

''You're a stinking liar,'' screamed Hooper.

Wilson did not reply in words. With his open hand he
slapped Hooper in the face and knocked him down. As he
scrambled to his feet, the Captain struck him again on the
other side of the face; then he stood back and waited. Hooper
slowly got to his feet. Then Evanhoe stepped between them.
He pushed Hooper back against the wall and turned to Wilson. ''No, Captain; you'll hurt your hand. Let me soften him
for you.''

Hooper suddenly picked up a chair and held it aloft. Now

he was mad and ready for a fight. "Now, blast you, you touch me once more and you'll get this." He shook the chair threateningly. "And if you reach for that gun I'll bat you over the head before your hand can get to it. The rougher you get, the worse it's going to be for you?"

Evanhoe knocked him down. Slowly Hooper got up and stood staring at him. As his head cleared, instead of trying to get away, Hooper advanced toward the two men.

"I'm not afraid of you, not either one of you. Now go on and hit me again. And as for you, Evanhoe, this is what I've got to say to you. You'd better walk backward for the rest of your life, because some night I'm going to come up behind you with a baseball bat and I'm going to take that wooden head of yours for a ball and pretend I'm diMaggio. A couple of wise cops, are you?" He was yelling now. "Think you've got it all worked out, do you? Captain Wilson, the music-loving captain. Know all about it, don't you? Did you ever hear of such a thing as a music lesson, you big stew? Don't you know they have music lessons on records? And you play them and play them till you know what you're playing? No, you wouldn't know that much, would you? Never thought, did you, that I might be practicing? Not you. This was a great scheme to fool you. Why, you poor addle-pated old idiot, a child could fool you. Look what happened right here in front of you— but you don't know what happened. Didn't you hear anything about the fellow who went down the cellar after the girl after they'd had a fight? No, you wouldn't hear that either. And if you did hear it you wouldn't know what to do about it. I'm guilty. Why? Because I play a fiddle. Did you ask the barkeep about the fight she had with the fellow who followed her down the cellar? You ain't got enough sense to talk to a barkeep. Did you talk to that floosie barfly? Did you ask her about it? She heard it and she knew what they were fighting about. Did you do any of those things a nine-year-old child would have done? Not you. You're a police captain. Well, enjoy it while you can, sucker, because you're through. You going to arrest me now?"

Neither of the men answered that question.

"All right," said Hooper, "I'm going back to my room and if you want me come and get me."

Neither Wilson nor Evanhoe tried to stop him, and after he had gone out Wilson said: "That's not a bad guy."

After a minute's thought Wilson pointed to the victrola on the table in front him. "Send somebody up to that man's flat and give him back his victrola. Then tell the officer to stay out in the hall and see that Hooper doesn't leave his flat. Then go over and get that Goldie. A barfly, eh? The old woman didn't say much about her. Well, we'll talk to her."

As Evanhoe left the room he passed an officer in uniform coming in.

"Fingerprints, Captain," said the newcomer.

"That's what I've been waiting for," said Wilson. "Let's have them. Sit down."

"These are the prints of everyone in the square. We've had ten men working on them and split them up." Then he laid a smaller pile on the other side of the table. "These are the ones we got from the Schultz house. I made these myself."

"Good work, son," said Wilson. He picked up the cards and glanced through them. "Well?" he said.

"It's a funny case, Captain, and the prints don't help much. Nothing seems to tally. Now here are two sets of prints on the door as you go into the cellar from the outside. One of them is easy enough—Ray Watson's. On the door knob they were. There's also a print of his hand on the top of the cellar stairs, on the wall. His right hand. You get the picture, don't you? He went into the room from the outside, then ran up the stairs and either tripped or stumbled on something; anyway, he rested his right hand on the wall as he got to the top of the cellar stairs."

"All right, go ahead. Where did he go then?"

"I can't tell how long he took, but eventually he got to the banisters. There's a print of his fingers there as if he were going upstairs, but he didn't go upstairs. Now here," went on the expert, picking out two cards, "are the prints of a woman's hand. It's the hand of the girl's mother. That's on the inside of the cellar door toward the edge. Then there are a lot of other prints, but they are old and terribly smudged and blurred, not much use. But here is a funny thing, Cap. You know how dusty a cellar floor is usually. I don't mean deep with dust, but there's always some dust. Footprints show—and they do now. But something else that is a lot more important shows too. Whoever killed that girl grabbed a broom and wiped out his footprints as he walked upstairs. He must have gone up backwards. Marks of the broom sweepings all over the place. Whether Watson did that or not, I don't know. But his footprints don't show on the stairs. I could see your footprints, Captain, as you came in from the street to where the girl was lying. That was clear enough. And footprints of the other officer who came in with you. It must have been Evanhoe, or was it Vallely? Kind of interesting to look at them, too; little bits of short steps you took when you first came into the cellar, then a long step as you reached the side of the girl. It's all clear up to that point from the door to the girl, then back to the door; anybody could read that. Watson's steps are there too, as far as where the girl's body was lying. Then they finished. That's a pretty important point against Watson too, Captain. Where did he go? He didn't go out the front door, the way you did. He went up the stairs, as his fingerprints show. But he didn't leave any footprints. The guy couldn't have flown. But if he killed the girl, then went up the steps backward, he might have swept up every trace of a footprint."

"He might have," said Captain Wilson.

"It's clear as far as it goes. But there's nothing to prevent us thinking that somebody else came down, found the girl, killed her, then swept up his footprints and Watson's too. You've got to consider that. Now the rest of the story is told very clearly. The murder is committed. The murderer is gone, Watson's footsteps on the stairs are gone too. Then the mother comes down into the cellar. She stands for a minute at the head of the cellar stairs, sees her daughter's body on the floor, runs down to it, kneels beside her for a minute, then up and out the front door.''

He pointed to the pile of photographs. "I got pictures of all that, Captain. That's what happened.''

About this time repercussions from the Captain's order restricting people to their homes in the square began to be heard. As old Mrs. Durkin told about it afterwards, all hell broke loose. Men, women and children surged into the room where Captain Wilson had made his headquarters. Women with market baskets on their arms, boys with schoolbooks; they all wanted to go away. It was a pandemonium of yelling and shouting.

"I got to go to market," shouted a woman.

"I got to go to school," said a boy.

"I'll lose my job," said a man. "You got no right to do this to us. I'm an American citizen, I demand my rights.''

Then into the hurly-burly barged a police sergeant. He didn't talk, he bellowed: "What's all this, what's all this?''

Captain Wilson looked at him coldly. "Did I send for you?'' he asked quietly.

"No," said the sergeant.

"Did you hear me call for help?''

"No, I didn't.''

"Then I suppose the Commissioner sent you.''

"No, Captain; no, sir.''

Then the Captain shouted: "Then get the hell out of here!'' He advanced a step toward the crowd. "And that goes for all the rest of you too.''

As the crowd filtered out through the doorway, Inspector Hunt faded in. He was in plain clothes, carrying a suitcase which he tossed over on the floor, and then Wilson saw him for the first time. He saluted formally—a captain saluting his superior officer.

Hunt, who was fat, waddled over to the Captain. "Well, Wilson! I was in London and heard you were having trouble, so I grabbed a plane and here I am. Funny thing about it, they wouldn't take me on board unless I had two tickets!

Selling places by the pound, I guess. So you've been having trouble, haven't you? Well, you've got a nice day for it. How you coming along? Cozy little place you've got here.''

At this Lieutenant Evanhoe, who had just come in, laughed. At the sound of his laughter Hunt gave a start but he didn't turn round. He stood facing the Captain. ''By golly,'' he said, ''I haven't heard that laugh in years. Don't tell me, don't tell me anything about it at all, but I never forget a good laugh. Wait a minute. Wait a minute. Now what was that cop's name! I know — Evanhoe!''

He turned and saw Evanhoe for the first time. ''By golly,'' he exclaimed, ''I was right again!'' And they shook hands. He stepped back a little and looked gravely at Evanhoe. ''Well, how are you, son? You look all right. How did you get that belly?''

''Meal by meal.''

''What are you now, Evanhoe? A roundsman? You've not got on a uniform, so how should I know?''

''No, Inspector. I'm a lieutenant of detectives.''

''Well, that's nice,'' said Hunt, and he turned to Wilson. ''Me and Evanhoe used to be buddies thirty years ago, back in the old Tenderloin.''

Evanhoe laughed at him. ''Oh, yes we were! You were a captain and I was a rookie.''

''Yes,'' said Hunt, ''that's true. And what a rookie! You wouldn't believe it, but that boy was good. Many's the time I've seen him staggering into the station house carrying five or six pails of hot coffee. And not spill a drop either. Well, we've not got cops like that any more.'' The old man fell into a chair and stretched out his legs. ''Nowadays if I ask a cop to go out and fetch me a cup of coffee you'd think I'd sent him to a precinct up in the Bronx, or something. How about one now, Evanhoe?''

''Coming right up with it now, sir. How about you, Captain?''

''No, thanks.''

As he went out Evanhoe said: ''That girl's name is Goldie

Newmark, and she'll be up in a few minutes, sir."

After the door closed Hunt climbed out of his chair, and as he did so Wilson came to meet him. Hunt put his hand on the Captain's shoulder and after a short pause said: "Well?"

"Boss, I can't wake up another morning to face another murdered girl. Did you see what the papers had in their editorials this morning?"

"I read every one," said Hunt. "What about it?"

"There's this about it. I went to the Commissioner this morning and offered to resign. That was before I came here at all. Then I come over here and there's another murder."

Hunt grinned at him. "They won't let you resign," he said. "Besides you're pretty old to get a new job. Being a detective is about everything you know, isn't it?"

"Yes," said Wilson, "that's true enough. But none of that knowledge is any good to me. I've tried everything."

"Son," said Hunt, "nobody's knowledge or experience is any good against the actions of a crazy man. That's the kind of man you can't outguess.

CHAPTER 10

YOUNG DR. WATSON WAS WORRIED, greatly worried, and as a man about to be married he was very properly talking the matter over with his girl.

"We have to face it, Mary," he said. "There's no use pretending I'm not in a mess. It's no use saying I'm innocent and that innocent men are not punished. I'm in a hell of a jam and you know it and I know it. If some time in the remote future we do get married I want you to promise me one thing. Don't let me make a fool of myself any more. I'm always doing it.

"I should have been there to watch over you," said Mary. "I could have prevented all this if I hadn't gone off to buy clothes! Why did you give her advice, Raymond?"

"Because I'm a blasted idiot. I can't mind my own business. I never could learn to mind my own business."

Mary grinned at him. "You were trying to save a human soul, darling."

"I made a mess out of it," said Raymond honestly. "I stuck my neck out. Minnie was nothing to me. I'd known Minnie ever since she was a little child and the minute she began talking wild about marrying the first fellow that came along, I lost my head. Why, when I think of the things I said to that girl, things that people heard! Things that I shouted at her! Why, Mary, I told her that I'd rather see her dead! I could have whispered that, couldn't I? But did I? Certainly not! You could have heard me a block away. I called her a bad woman. She slapped my face. Now there is just one thing a man can do when a woman slaps his face—"

"I didn't know that," said Mary. "What should he do?"

"Run. But did I? Oh no indeed. I went on with my sermon. And she slapped my face again. And even that didn't teach me. She dashed down the cellar and I had to go after her. Now I ask you! I ought to have my head examined."

"It's a beautiful head," said Mary. Then she became serious. "I don't have to tell you that I know you didn't do this, do I?"

"No, you don't have to tell me."

Mary was trying desperately to get him out of the mood he was in. "Of course I don't. I always told my mother that I'd never sit in a murderer's lap."

Then they kissed each other solemnly. When she could get her breath Mary went on, "What did you do when you got down in the cellar with her, dear? Did you speak to her at all?"

"Yes."

"What did you say to her?"

"I said I was sorry I had butted into her affairs, but that I was right about it."

"And what did she say to you?"

"She didn't say anything. She spat in my face. Then I turned and ran up the cellar stairs."

"And after that?"

"I came out into the street and wandered around."

Mary thought this over. "That doesn't seem very dangerous," she said finally.

"How can you tell? How can you tell? I opened the door to follow her in there. I closed the door after I was in there. And I know enough about police methods to know they've got those fingerprints. Yes, and they've got more. When I was running up the stairs from the basement I tripped and put my hand on that whitewashed wall at the top of the stairs. I might just as well have written, 'I went this way,' and signed it, 'Raymond Watson.' Mary, it's no use, there's no way I can explain it. You believe me because you're in love with me. Dozens of people saw me go down the cellar with Minnie. All the square heard us fighting. Dozens of people heard me say I'd rather she was dead."

"All right," said Mary, "that's that, isn't it? And that's the evidence against you so far. There's just one thing that's puzzling me about the whole thing. How are we going to get out of this mess so we can get married this afternoon?"

"We're not going to be married."

"Oh yes we are. Just the minute they let us out of this corral we're in. Got us locked up here like a lot of cattle. I'll have to have a talk with the Captain about this."

And at that very moment Captain Wilson was standing grinning at old Inspector Hunt in the room the police had reserved for their own use. Evanhoe had just come in carrying two pails of coffee, two cups and saucers, and a package of sugar. He drew up a chair and set it in front of Hunt.

"Seeing Evanhoe is pretty nice," said Hunt. "Brings back all the old days. My, they were good. Yes, sir, wonderful days."

Wilson was not much interested in old New York. He had his own troubles.

"Hadn't I better outline this case a little more fully?" he

said to the Inspector. "Don't you want all the facts?".

Hunt pretended not to hear him as he rambled on about his beloved old city. "Right around the corner from the station house was Sixth Avenue, only a couple of steps away; noisy, of course, but nice. The streetcars rattled and added to that was the roar of the elevated trains. Sometimes you'd hear a revolver shot, and the yells of some fellow who'd got hit over the head by a heavy-handed cop with a nightstick. Remember the nightsticks?"

Wilson shook his head.

"That's too bad, too bad," said the old man. "Where was I? Oh yes, on Sixth Avenue."

Evanhoe interrupted him. "Coffee, Inspector?"

"Yes," said Hunt, "sure. I was telling the Captain here about Sixth Avenue. You remember that, don't you, Evanhoe?"

"Yeah," said Evanhoe. "Paddy the Pig's."

"It all comes back to me, yes, sir. Right around the corner on 30th Street was Billy Gould's place. And down the Avenue another block was the Haymarket and gambling houses all over the place. And a couple of saloons on every street intersection."

He took a long deep drink of coffee. "My golly, that coffee's good," he said as he put down his cup. "Any sugar in it?"

"Four spoonfuls," said Evanhoe.

Hunt beamed at him. "What did I tell you about him, Wilson? Remembers everything. Son, the wife will kill you if she finds this out. Four spoonfuls of sugar! I only get half a spoonful at home. The wife has a crazy notion I'm getting fat." He took another deep drink of coffee. "That certainly is good. None of that funny coffee taste you find in the coffee you get most of the time these days. Well, Evanhoe, how much do I owe you?"

Wilson laughed at him. "This is on the house, Inspector."

"That's nice. That's the first time anybody has bought me anything in I don't know when. Not like the old days when a police inspector got things now and again. Why, there was a day not so long ago when nobody thought anything of giving an inspector a house and lot or a few shares of stock. Just between friends, you know. Little Old New York. There was a town for you. Nobody gives an inspector anything nowadays. Afraid they'll be arrested for giving a bribe. A fellow offered me a toothpick the other day in a restaurant and I said, 'How dare you bribe the police!' And, by golly, he thought I meant it.''

The door opened at this point and Goldie Newmark, wearing everything she had, and drenched with perfume, stood in the doorway smiling.

''Here's the Newmark girl,'' said Evanhoe. The old Inspector chuckled and sat back with a grin.

''Oh, come on in,'' said Wilson blandly.

She sank into a chair to which he pointed. Then he drew up another facing her. Goldie fluffed her hair a little and unconsciously Wilson ran his hand over his bald spot. ''Thank you for coming over so promptly,'' he said.

''It's a pleasure, I'm sure,'' said Goldie. In addition to her best clothes she had brought with her her best manners.

Hunt started to light a cigar, then stopped suddenly. ''Mind if I smoke, Miss Newmark?'' he asked.

Goldie was graciousness itself. ''Pray do,'' she murmured.

Hunt chuckled. ''Have you read that book *Upper Class Conversations?*'' he asked.

''No, I haven't. Is it good?''

''It's wonderful,'' said Hunt, solemnly. ''I read a chapter every morning.''

Wilson cut in suddenly: ''How would you like to tell me all you know about this murder?''

''Charmed, I'm sure.''

''It's only fair to warn you that you don't have to answer any of my questions if you don't wish to, and you can have a lawyer if you want one.''

Goldie giggled. ''I almost did, once, when I was working for one.''

''Minnie was a sweet girl,'' said Wilson, ''and she was brutally murdered. How would you like to help us catch the man who killed her?''

Goldie began to cry, and her manner and her mascara gradually went away. ''Sure I would,'' she said. ''Sure I'd like to help.''

''I thought you would. It was a terrible murder.''

''Don't I know it. He stuck his knife through a heart that was pure, pure gold, the—'' A sob took the place of an epithet.

Then Hunt cut in. He hadn't any use at all for what was going on. He leaned forward a little and said: ''Okay, Goldie, spill it!''

''Sure,'' said Goldie, ''where do I begin?''

''At the beginning,'' said Hunt.

''Well,'' started Goldie, ''I was born in the Bronx.''

Wilson interposed hastily. ''The Inspector means to start from this morning and go on from there.''

''I do hope they won't put my picture in the paper,'' said Goldie hopefully.

''Of course they'll want your picture,'' said Wilson wearily. ''Tell us what happened this morning.''

Then Hunt broke in again. ''I'm just a plain cop, Toots. Spill it.''

Goldie remade her mouth while the two policemen fumed quietly.

''Well, you see I was out of work and so was Minnie, poor dear. You see she'd never had a job, so it wasn't so bad for her. Anyway, we got talking about one thing and another, as girls do, and we found ourselves in Jimmy's place. We had a couple of drinks. Then Raymond Watson came into it somehow.''

''Now,'' said the Inspector, ''we're getting somewhere. Goldie, did anybody ever tell you how smart you are?''

Goldie started giggling. ''Oh, Inspector!''

''I don't mind telling you,'' said Hunt, ''that we trust your judgment. We think you're awfully smart. So I'm telling you confidentially that we're going to arrest Raymond Watson for this murder. You won't tell anybody, will you? I can trust you, can't I? Tell me that I can, Goldie.''

"God, yes, Inspector, to the last gasp.''

"Tell me something more about Watson. I hear he's a doctor, and somebody else says he's a taxi driver . . .''

"Well, both things are true. He just got made a doctor. He owns his own taxicab and drives that around nights to make money.''

"Oh, that's where he gets his money, is it?'' said Hunt. "I see. So you were talking things over with Minnie, talking about this and that, I mean. Then Watson came in, didn't he? And they had some sort of disagreement?''

"Yes, you could call it that. Anyhow, she slapped the be-jesus out of him.''

"Why did she do that?'' asked Wilson.

"Well, I don't know that I could blame her exactly. When Ray came in and spoke to us Minnie asked him to lend her ten dollars. And he dived into his pocket for it, but I guess he must be part Scotch because his hand was empty when it come out of his pocket. He wanted to know where she was going to get the ten to pay him back. Then for no reason at all he lost his temper and talked to her terribly and said that she would end up by being a tramp. After that, one word led to another and the doctor said she'd better come downtown to his clinic and see the women there. Now, wasn't that an awful thing to say to a girl, who was really contemplating matrimony? He called her names, so she slapped his face. Then he said he'd sooner kill her than see her wind up on the streets.''

"Wait a minute,'' said Wilson. "You're sure he said he would kill her?''

"Well, he didn't say, 'I'll kill you.' He said, 'I'd just as soon see you dead.' Same thing, isn't it?''

Wilson kept after her. "Do you remember exactly what he said?''

"Not exactly, maybe. Anyway, I wouldn't repeat it because it was a stinking thing to say to a lady. It must have hurt her like hell because she slapped his face two or three times after that.''

"What did he say to all that?" asked Wilson.

"I didn't hear everything. Suddenly she turned and ran into the cellar of her own house, and he followed her down through the cellar, slammed the door behind him, and then killed her."

Wilson held up his hand and she stopped talking for a minute. "How do you know he killed her?"

"Well, she's dead, isn't she?"

"This is very important," said Wilson. "We can take it that you can swear you saw him follow her down into the basement?"

"Yes, I did."

"How long did he stay there?" went on Wilson.

"I don't know. I'm a great hand for minding my own business. I thought maybe it was just a lover's quarrel, but I've been thinking about that. I don't know how it could have been a lover's quarrel really, because—" She stopped suddenly and looked from Hunt to Wilson. "You fellows really want a little help on this case?"

"We want a lot of help," said Wilson.

"Well, I've been thinking. I've got an idea, but it all depends on one thing. You know all those other murders?"

"Yes," said Hunt, "he does."

"Well then, was this one like them?"

"Yes, exactly like them," said Wilson. "No difference in any way."

"I'm glad you told me that, because that changes what I was thinking at first. You see, Inspector, what I thought was that this was a lover's quarrel and he sort of killed her in a jealous rage because she said she was going to try to string a guy along for his money. I hope I'm not butting in—"

"No," said Hunt, "you're illuminating."

"I get you. You mean I'm throwing a light on it."

"Yes," said Hunt, "that is exactly what I mean."

"Go on," said Wilson, "tell us some more."

"Well, here's the way I thought it out. It just came over me while I was sitting here. If this is like all the other cases, maybe he did them, too. Maybe he killed just for fun."

"Yes," said Wilson, "maybe he did."

"Sure he did," echoed Goldie. "Can't you see? He had his cab, he could go anywhere, just stop it, butcher some poor girl, and drive away."

"Thank you very much," said Wilson gravely.

Then Hunt added his bit: "I didn't know women could think so clearly."

"I don't want to take any credit for thinking," said Goldie. "It just came to me like a flash. I guess that's about all I could tell you two."

"You've been very useful," said the Captain.

Goldie swaggered toward the door. There she stopped and turned around. "Of course I understand it's the duty of every American citizen to do his duty, but there's no harm in my asking you if there's a reward?"

Hunt chuckled. "Don't you think the knowledge of a duty well done is reward enough, Goldie?"

"Well, when you're out of work and everything—"

As the girl went out she passed Evanhoe on his way in. He had a bundle of letters in his hand. As the door closed Wilson said: "Get me this fellow Watson right away, will you?"

"Yes, sir," said Evanhoe. Then he handed the letters to Hunt. "Your secretary sent these to you, sir. He said to tell you that somebody has laid an egg."

Hunt looked at the letters and found they had been opened. "Who read these?" he asked.

"Your secretary," said Evanhoe, and turned toward the door.

Hunt gave a quick glance at one letter, then he said: "We'd better wait a bit on this Watson thing. We've got something here."

CHAPTER 11

"FIRST OF ALL," SAID HUNT, turning to Captain Wilson, "you've been saying all along that this murderer was killing these girls because he hates you and is getting his revenge that way. Still think so?"

"Yes."

"Why?"

"There's no other explanation. What more do you want than what happened right here today? He wrote that unless I was fired the murders would continue and he pointed to Greenwood Square in the same letter. No connection at all between any of the girls. All murdered the same way under the same conditions—of course it's the work of one man."

"All right," said Hunt, "let's work on that hypothesis." He opened an envelope. "Now here's the first of this batch of letters. It's not a letter really, it's just a clipping from an editorial in one of the morning papers. No writing on it, see? But here is what it says: 'Captain Wilson's theory is that the murders are committed not for the delight in murder nor for any blood lust but solely to discourage him and bring about his leaving the department. We hope this theory is right, then the murders can be ended by removing him from the police department. No man's job is worth the lives of these young girls. It's too bad, but good-bye, Captain Wilson.' "

"I know," said Wilson, "I read that, and so did my wife, and so did my daughter."

Hunt leaned forward and placed four clippings on the table in front of Wilson.

"There you are, four of them," he said. "All the same. No writing. All addressed to me with a typewriter. Of course I can't be sure but it looks to me like the same typewriter."

"That's not what I want to see," said Wilson. "Let me see the envelopes."

"Atta boy," said Hunt. "The old bean is working again. Here they are."

Wilson looked at them very carefully. "They were all post-marked at three o'clock in the morning. Couldn't have been mailed much earlier because the paper wouldn't have been out long."

"Go on talking," said Hunt.

"Postmarked by Station E, Substation H, Substation S, and Substation R. Now who would be sitting up between one and three in the morning to read a *Gazette* editorial unless he expected to find something there?"

Hunt heaved himself to his feet and slapped Wilson on the back. "Son, we're getting somewhere," he said.

"Yes, I know, but wait a minute."

"You do the waiting, fellow. This old brain of mine is work-ing. Get me the editorial room of the *Gazette*," he said into the phone. "I want to talk to Roscoe Pierce. Say it's Tubby Hunt."

Presently he was talking to Editor Pierce as one old friend to another, asking how the editorial had come to be written, listening intently to the answer, and finally making a future lunch date. Then he cradled the phone and turned to Wilson. "Pierce says somebody phoned in the suggestion for that editorial."

"Somebody suggests the editorial?" said Wilson. "Then somebody cuts it out of the paper and mails four copies to you. Then somebody comes along and kills Minnie Schultz. That simplifies things, doesn't it? Find that somebody. And of course this same somebody mails all four copies inside of an hour. That's all the time he'd have to do it in, considering the time the first edition was out on the street. I wonder how far apart those four mailing stations are."

Wilson leaned over and picked up the phone. "Headquar-ters? This is Captain Wilson calling. I want to know some-thing about the location of several postal stations in New York and—never mind, I've got another way to find out."

Standing beside the table with the phone in his hand, he

had been looking out into the square and had seen Gus Smith, the postman, coming across it.

"Do you see what I see?" asked Wilson.

"As I live, a postman," said Hunt. "If he doesn't know, who does?"

Hunt walked to the window, threw it open and called out into the street: "Hey, you! Do you know a lot about where New York's postal stations are?"

A high-pitched, nervous voice came up to him: "Certainly I know where they are. Know all about 'em. What do you think I've been a postman all my life for? I've worked in most of them."

"That's great," said Hunt. "Come on in and help us out like a good fellow."

The postman came in. "Somebody in here want to see me?" he asked.

"Yes, I do," said Wilson. "Sit down."

"As the fellow says when they offer him a drink, I don't mind if I do. They offer us all sorts of things when we go the rounds. But nobody has offered me a chair in quite a while. What can I do for you?"

"You know who I am?" asked Wilson.

"Sure. And I got a lot of sympathy for you, too. And I want you to understand that if there's anything I can do to help, I'll be glad to do it."

"I thought you would be," said Wilson. "I want to know the exact location of these stations. There's Station E and Substations H, S, and R. Do you know where they are?

"Why, sure," said Smith. "I know where they are. Now E is where I work. It's about half a block away from here. But H is about four miles away, out on Ninth Avenue."

Wilson said encouragingly "That's what we want to know. How far apart are all these stations?"

Hunt said: "What we want to find out is, could a man go to all these stations inside of an hour?"

"Well, then he'd go from S to R. To do that he'd have to go to First Avenue, then up about thirty blocks—no, I'm wrong, I guess it'd be easier to go right straight up—no—"

"All we want to know," said Hunt, "is how far it is—about. You don't have to be entirely accurate. About how far would he have to go?"

"Well," said Smith, "call it thirteen miles, and I don't believe any postman in the world could do it in an hour, lugging a heavy pack and all."

"I didn't say anything about a postman," said Hunt.

Smith laughed a little. "I know you didn't, I know you didn't. But I had to work it out the way it would come to me. I'm a postman and I'm telling you the way I'd do it."

"I can understand that," said Hunt. "Thirteen miles to walk in an hour for a fellow to do with a mailbag on his shoulder is quite a stunt, isn't it?"

"Yes, it is," said Smith.

"Suppose," interposed Wilson, "he took a streetcar or a taxi?"

"Yes, I hadn't thought of that. Of course he could go in a taxi or in a streetcar. That all you want?"

"Yes," said Wilson. "We just wanted to get those distances."

"All right." Smith got up and settled the strap of his bag on his shoulder. He started toward the door and then stopped. "I hope you won't think I'm fresh if I ask you something."

"No," said Wilson, "shoot, what is it?"

"Well, it's about that stuff in the *Gazette* this morning. I think that was sort of a stinking thing to do to you. You're not liable to lose your job if you don't catch this fellow, are you?"

Hunt said "What kind of a department do you think the police department is? You're working under Civil Service just the same as we are, aren't you? Would they fire you because you made a mistake?"

"No, they wouldn't. No, sir, all you got to do in our department is vote Democratic." He laughed as he moved toward the door. "Well, good luck to you boys. Good afternoon all." He closed the door softly behind him.

"Kind of a nice man at that," said Hunt.

Then from the street came the sound of the postman's laughter, light and gay.

"Sort of stuck on his own jokes, isn't he?" said Hunt. "Must have thought that Democratic joke kind of funny. Now, how about those letters? Suppose he started at Station E, where would he hire a taxi to make that trip?"

"Wait a minute," said Wilson, "wait a minute. Watson wouldn't have had to hire a cab."

"Well, by golly," said Hunt, "I hadn't thought of that. He could use his own and go where he wanted to and it wouldn't have to show on the meter either."

"Evanhoe, get me Watson," said Wilson sharply. And Evanhoe went.

There was a long uneasy pause. Hunt got up, walked over to the window, looked out for a minute, came back again, settled himself with a groan into his chair. Finally he said to Wilson: "Son, there's something wrong about this, something terribly wrong."

"What's wrong?" said Wilson.

"It's too easy," said Hunt, "too darned easy."

Presently the door opened and Watson came into the room. Mary was with him and so was Evanhoe, who stood behind them with his back to the door. Hunt beamed on them.

"You sent for me, Captain Wilson?" said Watson.

"Yes, I did," said Wilson. "Funny thing our meeting again this way, isn't it? I don't suppose you're married yet, are you?"

"No we're not," said Mary, "and that's your fault, Captain. We were planning to get married this afternoon, but you won't let us get out of here."

"Well, well, that's too bad," said Hunt. "Everything arranged for the wedding?"

"Yes," said Mary.

"Time set?" asked Hunt.

"Yes."

"Well," went on Hunt. "I'll tell you what I'll do for you.

If there's no arrest and everything's as it is now, how would you like me for your best man, to go along with you and bring you back safely here again? It's kind of bad luck for a wedding to be postponed. But if I do that for you, young fellow, I think you ought to help me out if you can.''

"I'll help you out in any way I can," said Watson.

"Well, there's something I don't understand about this wound, and you're a doctor, so perhaps you could explain it to me."

"Yes, I can do that. I'm getting a little used to doing that," he said, laughing a little. "About ten days ago Captain Wilson pulled Mary and me into a station house, and all we'd been doing was kissing in my cab. I hadn't seen her in a couple of weeks and I thought I was entitled to a couple of kisses. And then he asked the same question as you're asking, Inspector. How can you stab a girl in the heart and not make her bleed? You remember that, Captain?"

"Yes," said Wilson, "and I'll explain it later to the Inspector. I might as well tell you, Watson, that this is a little more serious. If you want a lawyer here you can have one."

"I don't want a lawyer."

"You know you don't have to answer any of my questions."

"Yes I know. And I know that anything I say can be used in evidence against me. But, Captain, I'm quite willing to tell you anything I can. And I'm going to tell you one thing right at the start, too. If you think I had anything to do with the killing of Minnie Schultz, you're crazy. After all, look at it from my point of view for a minute."

Wilson said: "I'm going to do the questioning."

"I know. I know that. And I'm going to do the answering. But before we start I want you just to look at Mary there. I want you to bear in mind that we're in love with each other and have been for three years. And we'd planned to be married this afternoon. That's all clear, isn't it?"

"Yes," said Wilson, "that's clear. But what isn't clear is why you killed Minnie Schultz."

"I didn't."

"Well, son," interposed Hunt, "let's talk about it a little. Let's see what we can find out. Wilson thinks you did. And I've got kind of a notion that you did. Wouldn't you like to know why we think so?"

"Yes, I would, because it seems sort of — oh, what's the use of discussing it. You ask me the questions and I'll answer the best way I know how."

"Suppose I start the ball rolling," said Hunt. "I've got one or two things I'd like to know about. Dr. Watson, how long have you known Captain Wilson here?"

"I don't know him at all. I had that one little adventure with him that you know about, and that's all."

"Had you seen him before that time?"

"Not to my knowledge."

"I hope you're not one of those fools who say that all cops look alike to them."

"No," said Watson, "I'm not. And I hope you're not having fun with me, Inspector, or anything of that sort. I'm here to answer your questions the best way I know how, and the sooner we get down to cases the better. Perhaps it will help you to know that I had a row with Minnie Schultz this morning."

"We knew about that," said Wilson.

"Why did you have a row with her?" asked Hunt.

"Because I'm a crazy fool. Never can mind my own business, not for a minute."

"Wait a minute," said Mary. "I expect I'm to blame for some of that. You see, instead of staying around with Raymond the way I ought to have today, I went shopping. He hasn't started his practice yet. He had only just put up his sign at our front door, and he didn't have anything to do. If I'd been here when Goldie and Minnie called to him, he wouldn't have gone with them, or if he had I'd have gone too. We've known those girls for years. Go on, dear, tell them the rest of it."

"Just a moment," said Hunt, "there's a question I want to put in here. Dr. Watson, right after the girl's body was found, why didn't you tell the Captain you had had a row with her and that you'd been down the cellar? Why the secrecy?''

"Why didn't I tell?" said Watson. "How many times do I have to tell? I told him once, not three minutes after the murder was discovered. I told him all that."

"Why did you do that?" asked Hunt.

"Why shouldn't I do it?" said Watson. "It was the truth."

"Yes," said Wilson, "it was the truth. But you didn't tell me what went before that. You didn't tell me why you'd followed her down."

"Because," said Watson, "you told me that was all you wanted to know and you would talk to me later on."

"So I did, and now I'm talking to you."

"What was this row about?" asked Hunt suddenly.

"I don't know if I can make you quite understand it," said Watson. "In the first place, let me tell you that I am the kind of a man who never minds his own business. If I had had any sense I would have walked away from her. But I didn't. She was a silly kid and when she told me she was going to get money by stringing fellows along I told her she was a fool and she slapped my face."

"Goldie Newmark overheard that, didn't she?" said Wilson.

"Yes, she did."

"I'm going to explain this to you," said Wilson, "so you'll understand what we really have." He pointed to a pile of papers on the table in front of him. "We have microphones in this room which pick up everything that is said. Here is a transcription of what she said, in typewriting. The reason we have this is because eventually we'll have it sworn to and it might be used as evidence in case Goldie should change her mind or something. I am telling you this very frankly."

"I see," said Watson.

"Now," said Wilson, "this is what Goldie said. Mind you, this is her own statement. Here it is: 'He lost his temper and talked to her terribly. He called her names, so she slapped his face.' Suppose you tell us what you said to her, Watson."

Watson said nothing.

The Captain went on. "Well, quoting Miss Newmark again:

'It was a stinking thing to say to a lady. It must have hurt her like hell because she slapped his face two or three times.' ''

Wilson picked up another sheet of paper. ''Goldie says, and again I am quoting: 'He said ''I'd just as soon see you dead.'' Suddenly she ran down into the cellar and he followed her and killed her.' Then I said to Goldie: 'How do you know he killed her?' ''

Wilson paused for a minute before continuing: ''And what do you think Goldie said to me in reply to that? She said she saw Minnie hit you in the face, she heard the row, she heard every word you both said, and she saw you follow Minnie down into the cellar.''

And to this Watson said nothing.

Finally Hunt spoke: ''Watson, Goldie Newmark said that you followed this kid into the cellar, and that you killed her. How about that?''

''I did follow her into the cellar, but I didn't kill her.''

There followed a long pause. Wilson was clearly waiting for something. Twice he looked at his watch nervously. Watson sat looking from one to the other, and Mary sat looking at him. Suddenly she leaned forward and kissed him. And then she said with a little laugh: ''I did that because he's such a sweet lamb.''

The silence in the little room was oppressive. Outside the noises went on. Small boys shouting. High-pitched voices of women laughing and talking. The general clatter of a summer day blown in with the acrid smell of the city.

Then the thing Captain Wilson had been waiting for happened. The door was opened and Minnie Schultz's mother came in. A woman of fifty, thin, her face tear-stained, her sandy gray hair disheveled. She stood for a minute in the door and all she saw was the Captain, and she went towards him at once.

''Excuse me, please, Captain. I know I don't look so good. I ain't had time to tidy up. I've been trying to get something ready to wear for tomorrow.''

Suddenly Mary moved her chair closer to Watson's and put

a protecting arm across his shoulders. Then, for the first time, Mrs. Schultz noticed the two young people.

"So," she said, and she picked up a chair and planted it in front of the Captain's. And after a pause she went on. "Was there something I could tell you, Captain?"

"Yes," said Wilson, "there are a good many things you could tell me perhaps. You were at home when you called out to Minnie about the jam?"

"Sure."

"What did you do after that?"

"Well, after that, I went back to my work. By-and-by, when Minnie don't come up, I say to myself, darn that lazy good-for-nothing — and all the time, oh my God — when I was saying that, I should go on, Captain?"

"Please," said Wilson.

"Well," said Mrs. Schultz, "when she don't come I go down to the basement, and all the way down I keep saying to myself, 'My God, and I have to do everything for myself,' and when I get there, oh my God, oh my God, oh my God — then I see her lying there. First of all, I don't know what is the matter. Then I run down them little steps and I kneel beside her and I give her a little shake. Then I find out."

She turned to the Captain again. "Please, Mister, please don't make me say nothing more. Mister, who killed my Minnie?"

CHAPTER 12

MRS. SCHULTZ WAS CRYING: "Mister, who killed my Minnie? Who killed my Minnie?" Captain Wilson, to whom she was speaking, moved closer to her. "Mrs. Schultz, if you want to know about your daughter's death, ask Watson."

"He knows?" said Mrs. Schultz. "Then tell me."

"I don't know," said Watson.

"The mister there says to ask you. You know I got to know, don't you?"

"I don't know who killed her. I swear to you I don't know." Then Watson turned to the Captain and said furiously: "Captain, you can't do this to her. I've known Mrs. Schultz ever since I was a kid. And I'm not going to tell her what her daughter said. I haven't any right even to ask her to hear it."

Wilson turned toward the microphone and said "Mike, have you got the notes on what Watson has said in this case?"

Mike stamped on the floor to show that he had.

"Then come on down and read them to us here."

Watson said: "Hasn't she suffered enough? What's the use of reading them to her?"

Then, in a flat voice, Mrs. Schultz said: "I want to hear."

Notebook in hand, Mike entered and sat down.

Wilson said: "I want you to read —"

Mrs. Schultz," Watson interrupted, "please don't listen to this. We don't know what really has happened. There are things people have said and they aren't true!"

"So?" said Mrs. Schultz.

Wilson came over and put his hand on Watson's shoulder. "All right, young fellow, tell us the truth. Did you kill Minnie?"

"No."

"Read your notes," said Wilson, turning to the policeman.

The policeman cleared his throat, opened his notebook. "In response to a question, Watson said — and I am quoting: 'She told me she was going to get money by stringing fellows along.' "

Mrs. Schultz shrieked: "No, my Minnie didn't! I'm her mother, I'd know!"

The policeman went on: "I'm still quoting Watson. 'I told her she was a fool and she slapped my face.' "

Mrs. Schultz stared from one to the other. "My Minnie did that?"

Captain Wilson said: "Read what Goldie Newmark said. Maybe that will make her believe it."

Mike turned the pages of his notebook. "This is what Goldie said, and I quote: 'He said "I'd just as soon see you dead" and she slapped his face two or three times.' "

"Ya! So?" said Mrs. Schultz.

Then the dull voice of the policeman went on again: " 'Then she ran down into the cellar and he followed her.' "

"Wait a minute," said Mrs. Schultz. "You got that in the book there?"

"Yes," said the policeman.

Mrs. Schultz turned to Watson. "You did that? You went into the cellar after my Minnie?"

"Yes."

Mrs. Schultz came closer to him. "You went down the cellar after my poor Minnie?"

"Yes. I wanted to tell her something. She wouldn't listen. I saw it wasn't any good, so I came away."

"You didn't hit her or anything?"

"No, Mrs. Schultz, I didn't go near her."

"You didn't go near her?"

"Before God I didn't."

Then Mrs. Schultz screamed and through the screams came the words: "Liar! Liar! Liar!" She turned to the Captain. "He killed my Minnie. He killed my Minnie. Now I know it. Why would he lie to me if he didn't kill her. He says he didn't go near her."

"And that's the truth — I didn't."

The old woman sobbed and screamed and suddenly she tore at the buttons on her dress and thrust her hand into her bosom. She brought out an envelope and held it toward the Captain.

"He didn't go near her, he swears. And beside my little girl, when I get on my knees by her, I find this. Look where it says his name! His letter beside my Minnie."

Wilson said: "I'll take that."

He held out the letter toward Watson. "It's addressed to you, isn't it, Watson?"

"Yes."

"How do you think it came to be beside the body of Minnie

Schultz? How are you going to answer that question?"

"I don't know."

"I suppose it walked there by itself."

Watson yelled at him: "I suppose you think I killed the girl and left my calling card, eh?"

Mrs. Schultz kept on screaming: "He killed my Minnie! He killed my Minnie!"

Then Hunt said: "Evanhoe, we'd better take her upstairs." He got up out of his chair and patted her on the shoulder. "Now, now, that's all right, Mother," he said. "We'll look after you. If he killed your Minnie, he'll pay for it."

The sobbing woman was half carried and half led out of the room. Then Hunt came back and stood beside Watson. "Got anything to say?" he asked him.

"What can I say?"

"Can you explain the letter?" asked Hunt.

"I can't," said the boy. "I've told you all I know about the case, everything."

Then Hunt changed his line of questioning. "What have you got against Captain Wilson?"

"Nothing. I've only seen him twice in my life. He'll tell you that."

Wilson suddenly shouted at him: "And why did you kill the other girls too?"

And Watson shouted back: "I didn't kill anybody."

"All right," said Wilson, "that's what I wanted to know." And, turning to Evanhoe, who had just returned to the room, he said:

"Those are Watson's fingerprints, Evanhoe. Take all this downtown. See what they can find on the envelope and tell them for God's sake to hurry."

A policeman came into the room quietly. He was white and a little breathless. "It's the Commissioner," he said. "He's talking like a crazy man." And he stepped aside to let Commissioner Doyle come into the room.

Doyle stopped for a minute in the doorway and frowned at the men in the room. Then over his shoulder he barked at the policemen crowded in the hallway outside. "Nobody comes in here. Nobody." He slammed the door behind him and stood and faced the other two. To Wilson he gave a nod. "How are you, Hunt?" he said to the Inspector. Then he glared from one to the other.

"So you've got them all bottled up, have you Wilson? Murderer is right here in this little square."

"Yes," said Wilson, "he is."

"That's good," said Doyle. "That's fine. Then how was he able to phone me from a public booth in the Times Building over an hour ago?"

"Oh no," said Wilson, "no."

"Captain, I'm getting used to that man's voice. There's no question about it. That was the man."

Wilson didn't wait to get to the door. He simply turned and threw open the window and shouted out into the square: "Evanhoe! I want Evanhoe to come back." Then he slammed down the window and turned back to the Commissioner. "What did he say to you, Commissioner?"

"You know that queer high-pitched voice he's got. Sounds a little as if he were trying to conceal his voice, speaking in a falsetto, and this time it was pretty definite what he wanted. He said to me: 'Get rid of Wilson. And I don't mean next week, next month or next year, I mean now. I want charges against him that will send him out disgraced for life. And this is not a request either. You're getting orders, Commissioner. And there's only one way you can stop me, and you'd better do it.' And that's the way he spoke to me over the phone — to me, the Police Commissioner! Wilson, I want that fellow."

"Yes, I know."

"I'm glad you do. And that doesn't mean the day after to-morrow either."

Evanhoe came in quietly. He saluted formally when he saw the Commissioner.

"Evanhoe," said Wilson, "the Commissioner had a telephone message from our murderer an hour or an hour and a half ago. The fellow phoned from a public booth in the Times

Building. How did he get out of this square?"

"I don't believe he did," replied Evanhoe.

"My God," said the Commissioner, "don't you suppose this department has enough brains to know where a message came from? I tell you he phoned from the Times Building. How do you know he didn't get out of here?"

"Because," said Evanhoe, "nobody could get out of here. This place is bottled up tight. If he were a bird and could fly he might have gone off the roof. Otherwise he couldn't get out."

"I see," said the Commissioner. "If that's the case, then you never had him in here at all. If Evanhoe is right, if this place is bottled up and no one goes in or out, your murderer was out an hour and a half ago. Now what are you going to do?"

Before either of the men could answer, Mrs. Durkin's voice was heard, loud, shrill, terror-stricken. "Help, help! Police!"

Evanhoe was out of the room before anyone could give him orders. The Commissioner rushed to the window and looked out.

"They've gone crazy out there. Stark, raving crazy," he said. "They're running around like a lot of maniacs."

He threw open the window and the roar of the crowd surged into the room. And high above the other screams was heard the old woman's cries: "He's got Goldie! He's got Goldie!"

By now police whistles were blowing and there were more shouts. Then there was a thumping and a clumping in the hallway as though a heavy body were being dragged across the floor. Suddenly the door was thrown open, and there was Mrs. Durkin on the floor, still sobbing and screaming. "I saw him! I saw him do it!"

She stopped for breath and shouted: "You fools going to leave me on the floor all night?"

Doyle picked her up and put her into a chair. "Where's Captain Wilson?" she said. "I want Wilson. Got a lot to tell Wilson."

"I'm the Police Commissioner," said Doyle, "and this is

Inspector Hunt. Wilson has gone to investigate the case.''

"What's he got to investigate?" she shouted. "I saw it. I can tell. Goldie's room is right across the way from mine. I can see into her room. I saw her when she come out from here. And I saw her when she went to her own room. She stood at her window and waved to me. And I waved back at her. Then she went away, and I didn't see her for quite a while. I guess she must have changed her dress, because she came back to the window and lit a cigarette and I lit one too and we waved at each other, kind of friendly. Then there was a knock on the door — I guess there was, I didn't hear it. But I did hear her say: 'Come on in,' then she kind of laughed — you know how you do when you see someone you know coming into the place — and she walked toward the door. But before she got very far — oh my God, I saw it! I saw it happen. I just saw a man's arm with a long thin knife in his hand. And he stuck it into her heart. And I was scared and so excited that I fell out of my chair. And I started calling for help. Then they was all running toward Goldie's house, I guess, so I slid along the floor and fell down the stairs because I had to tell the Captain.''

"Yes," said the Commissioner. "Of course you did. Could you see anything more than the arm?"

"No, sir, I couldn't. Just the arm and the hand and oh my God, the knife! I could see that. And it come so quick, Goldie couldn't scream. There wasn't a sound.''

"And all you saw," went on the Commissioner, "was the man's arm and his hand, and of course the knife?"

"Yes, sir, that's all I saw.''

"Could you tell from that distance what color his coat was?"

"Yes, it was a sort of a gray. But it couldn't have been him. No, sir. He's too nice a fellow.''

"Who's the nice fellow?"

"Why, young Watson. He was wearing a coat of that color today. But it couldn't have been him. What reason would he have to do it? She was always a good friend of his.''

CHAPTER 13

THERE WAS NO CLUE EXCEPT what Mrs. Durkin said, in the murder of Goldie Newmark; no fingerprints were found either on the door or near the door. No one had seen any stranger walk into the house or come out of it. There was an investigation carried on under the eyes of the Police Commissioner himself and of Inspector Hunt too. Every flat in the square had been searched, not in a perfunctory way but by experts. Policewomen had been sent for and every woman in the square had been searched. They were looking for the weapon with which the girl had been killed. Every man had been stripped. And still no knife had been found. Monahan had accompanied the police from flat to flat. No one was in the square who did not belong there.

There had first been the search through Goldie's house, and when that was unavailing, when nothing was found there, Police Commissioner Doyle had every man, woman and child in the square called out of their houses and he talked to them. He seemed to speak with great frankness and this is what he said:

"In a time of great emergency for the police, as in this instance, we must call upon you citizens for help. Many of you have no idea who I am. For your information and to aid you perhaps in planning your actions for the next day or perhaps two days, let me tell you that I am the Commissioner of Police of New York. My name is Doyle. As you know, there has been a series of murders of young girls in this city which — well, the first murder took place five or six weeks ago and there have been too many of them and we have not caught the murderer. Then this morning two girls, whom you all know, have been killed. Minnie Schultz was killed early this morning, that you know about. And about fifteen minutes ago Goldie Newmark was brutally butchered in her room.

"We have every reason to believe that the murderer has

not made his escape, and in order to capture him it has been necessary to ask everyone who lives in this square to remain in their own homes until such a capture is made. I want you to regard this square as a place under siege during a time of war. No messages can come in and none can go out. I am going to ask you not to use your telephones. It is very important that the news of this second murder should not be made public. So if you will all go back to your own homes, we will try and work this thing out as quickly as we can and with as little interference to all of you as posible. I am going to add one more thing, and that is that families in which young girls live guard those girls. Don't let them out and don't let people come in to see them. I can promise you that this trouble won't last very long. Now if you will go back to your houses, the police will go to work.''

Then Doyle stamped off and made his way into the building where the police were working and slammed the door after him.

Naturally the first thing some people did on getting back to their houses was to try to telephone for aid. The phones didn't work. In fact every telephone connection with the outside world — except the police phones — had been cut, and a length of wire eight or ten feet long had been removed so there was no way of repairing the cut.

So the isolation of the square began.

Then an ambulance from Bellevue was driven rapidly into the square. Goldie's body was put on a stretcher and rushed down to the Morgue at Bellevue for an autopsy.

The police do not think of everything. Neither Doyle nor Hunt nor Wilson said anything to the driver of the ambulance or the men carrying the body out to it. So the Commissioner's nice speech and all the cutting of wires and every precaution to keep the thing secret were no use at all. Inside of an hour extras were out. Boys screamed through every street in New York about the second murder in Greenwood Square.

Before the investgation had gone far the Mayor appeared in the unfurnished room that was being used as Little Headquarters by Doyle, Hunt, and Wilson. He had never been noted for an even temper. Today he was grim. He did not even come forward into the room at first. He stood in front of the door he had slammed behind him, with his little legs straddled apart, and it was a question which stuck out further, his stomach or his chin.

"I don't want any excuses," he said. He spoke very slowly and for him very coldly. "I know what you're up against. And maybe you know what I'm up against. Any way you look at it, it's a hell of a mess. Up to now it has got us all licked. Doyle, you have been Commissioner of Police here for four or five years. How many times have I interfered in your work? How many times have I given you orders to do this or do that?"

"Why, never," said the Commissioner.

"All right. Now I'm going to. We're going to put a radio broadcasting station right here in this square. In one of the rooms upstairs if you want it, and as a public service there will be an hourly broadcast of what is happening here. Best advertisement our city could have. All over the country people are yelling to have news about this thing, and they will have to tune in and get New York's own station to get it. Now that's the first advantage. Am I right or am I wrong?"

Doyle said: "There will be a good many things we can't let them know."

"All right, don't give them out. Nobody's telling you what to give them. But we want news of this case broadcast every hour on the hour, and I'll get the best broadcaster I can.

"And here is something else you gentlemen may not have thought about. Suppose you want to get something over to the murderer; you can't do it now because you can't reach him. You think you've got him in this square. I don't think you have. But if news is being broadcast every hour and he can get to a radio that's where he's going to be, whether he's in the square or out of the square. See the value of that."

"Well," said Doyle slowly, "it's different, anyhow."

"It's different," said the Mayor, "and it's durned good. And I want it done. I'll attend to that part of it, and you attend to yours. That's all I've come here to say. Goodbye."

He turned, and like a shot was out of the place and on his way down to the City Hall.

Before the investigators could make up their minds definitely as to where to start and whom to question first, Evanhoe came in. "That postman," he said, "that Gus Smith wants to know if he could talk to you a minute."

"Yes," said Doyle, "he can. Wait a couple of minutes, then bring him in."

As Evanhoe closed the door behind him, Doyle turned to the other two and said: "Now boys, here's where I fade out of the picture. I'll stay here because I'm so interested I couldn't stay anywhere else. But it's the Captain's show — and of course Hunt's. So, boys, go to it." And he took up a chair, set it against the wall, tilted it back and sat listening. Then Evanhoe brought in Gus Smith.

For a moment or two no one spoke. Wilson pointed to a chair, and Smith sat down, first having taken off his mailbag and rested it on the floor between his knees.

"What did you want to see me about?" began Wilson.

"The same old thing. The other day when that other girl was killed —"

"That was not any other day, that was this morning."

"My God," said the postman, "so it was, so it was this morning. Well, anyhow you told the cops outside not to let anybody out. That's all right, that's your business. Then you told them that that order did not go for the U. S. mails, and I guess that was pretty right too. But what do you want to do about it now? I've got my work to do. I've got my route to cover. I just started out a few minutes before this other affair happened, and I was stopped for fair. But that was all right with me. Yes, sir, if you tell Monahan to give me a room and a tub of hot water and two cups of washing soda and a good book, why you can keep me here as long as you darn please. But you'd better send word to the postmaster or somebody that the mails have been held up."

"There are one or two questions," said Hunt, "I'd like to

ask you. You know how it is, Gus. You don't mind my calling
you Gus, do you?"

"Hell no," said Smith, "why should I?"

"We've got your address; we have the address of everybody connected with this case. How long have you been living
at that address?"

"About three years."

"You married?" asked Wilson.

"No. I'm a widower."

"How long have you been on this route?"

"I don't know. I mean I don't know exactly. But it's over
a year."

"You must get to know the people along your route pretty
well, don't you? You must know a lot about most of them?"

"If you're trying to find out whether I read the postcards
coming to them, I don't."

"I don't mean that," said Wilson. "But a fellow like you
going around from house to house delivering mail for a year
and a half, must get to know the people very well."

"Yes I do," said Smith, "as a matter of fact. Now let's
take this little thing killed this morning."

"Minnie Schultz? What about her?"

"There's nothing that I know about her. She's been playing
around with the boys; just a fresh kid, you know, that's all.
No harm as far as I know."

"Here's what we're trying to get from you," interposed
Hunt. "Can you think of anybody who would want to kill her?
Was there any reason to get her out of the way?"

"Oh," said the postman, "I see what you mean. I see just
what you mean. Well, there's nothing I ever heard of. You
know how it is with those young girls. They just bat around.
No real reason for them to be here or anywhere else. As I
figure it out, a girl like that, if she gets married, has a couple
of brats, keeps her house kind of clean, and gives her husband
a companion — well, she's doing all that the good Lord meant
for her to do. Needn't have any brains. But as for being a girl
that anybody would want to kill, well it's silly, that's all."

"That's the way you look at it?" said Wilson.

"As long as you asked me," said the postman, "we've all got our opinions about men and women — what's a good man, what's a good woman. I can't see any difference whether she lived or died, but certainly there was no reason to kill her, no more than there was any reason for her to get born. That's my philosophy anyhow."

"That's very interesting," said Wilson, "very interesting. I don't suppose you ever heard anybody make any threats against her."

"No, I never did."

"And you can't think of any reason why anybody would want to kill her?"

"No, I can't."

"Well, that's that," said Hunt. "Now, then, Gus, how many letters did you deliver to Goldie Newmark today?"

"I didn't deliver any. There wasn't any at all. Anyway, most of these houses have letter boxes, and if there had been a letter for her I would have dropped it into the box with her name on it."

"How about this man Watson?" Hunt asked. "How did he get his mail?"

"Oh, he had a letter box."

"He always got his mail there?"

"Sure, unless I ran into him in the street and he said, 'Got any mail for me, Gus?' And I'd give it to him."

"How often did that happen?"

"I wouldn't know."

"I see. Well, let's take this morning as an example. How many letters did you have for the doctor this morning?"

"Three or four."

"What kind of letters were they?"

"I wouldn't know."

"What did you do with them? Did you give them to him or did you drop them in his box?"

"I dropped them in his box."

"About what time was that?"

"Along about nine o'clock. They came in on the first de-livery."

"That's all you had for Watson today?"

"Yup, that was all."

"Well, I guess that about covers it," said Hunt.

"Yes," said Doyle, "that settles it." He let his chair down and coming to the table shook hands with Smith. "Thanks a lot, Gus," he said. "We don't need you now. On your way."

"Just what does that mean?"

"You've got letters to deliver, haven't you?"

"Sure. There's something I would like to say, Commis-sioner, if you don't mind. I'm just as much interested in find-ing out who did these murders as you are. I'm ready to do anything you want me to to help, and if you have an idea I'm mixed up in this case, all you got to do is to say so."

CHAPTER 14

EVANHOE CAME IN HURRIEDLY and he was grinning.

"What's funny about this case?" asked Wilson.

"Well," said Evanhoe as he walked up to the table, "I think these are kind of funny. Anyhow, they might mean some-thing." He threw on the table a pair of thin black rubber gloves, men's gloves.

"By golly," said Hunt, "where did you find those?"

"Up in Watson's room."

"Oh," said Hunt, "you've been searching his rooms again, have you?"

"Yes. I went through them again just for luck."

"Did he make a fuss about it?" went on Hunt. "Did he object?"

"He wasn't there. There wasn't anybody there."

Hunt started to complain. "This is all wrong and I know it. My God, I haven't been a cop all these years for nothing. If he used rubber gloves for these murders you don't suppose he'd leave them lying around the place, do you?"

"They were right by the kitchen sink."

"All right. A guy wears rubber gloves because he doesn't want his hands to be mussed up, and now we know who committed the murders."

Evanhoe flushed angrily. "I didn't say anything about him committing the murders, Inspector. I went through his flat again like any good cop would have and I found these gloves. And that's that."

"See what you can get from the Bureau of Identification," said Hunt.

Evanhoe picked up the phone and talked rapidly to Police Headquarters while the others waited.

"There's plenty of fingerprints on that letter," he said, as he hung up the receiver, "and a lot of them can't be identified. They got the postman's, and a smudged thumb mark of the fellow that racks the letters in the cancellation machine. They made an identification of that. It appears some of them fell down and he had to pick them up and put them into the machine. And they've got the mark of the man who sorted them before he handed them over to Smith."

"What about Watson's?" asked Hunt.

"Nothing about Watson," said Evanhoe. "There's nothing to show he ever had had the letter or that it was ever given to him." He leaned forward and picking up the rubber gloves held them for a moment, then dropped them on the table. "This might explain it," he added.

"All right," said Hunt, "get Watson, bring him in and let's question him."

And that's what they did. But it was a different Watson this time, a blazing Watson accompanied by the girl he was going to marry. Before anyone could speak, he started. He turned to Captain Wilson again. "Listen," he said, "you're a police captain and you've got a lot of power and authority in this town, and I haven't any. Now get this into your head once and for all. I'm not a murderer. You arrested me once because

I was kissing my girl. You yanked me out of my own cab and brought me into the police station. My name was in all the papers, suspected of murder. Well, I forgave you that. And now you're after me again. Who have I killed this time? Is it the same old story — Minnie Schultz?''

"No," said the Captain, "it's not Minnie Schultz alone, it is Minnie Schultz and Goldie Newmark, too."

Watson began to shout. "Well, if that isn't the limit."

"Wait a minute, son," said Hunt, "wait a minute. Let's keep calm and cool about this. There's quite a lot of evidence against you. You had plenty of reason for wanting her out of the way after what she told us this morning. And she was killed in exactly the same way as all the others. It don't look so good for you. Now if you've got anything you can tell us that's going to straighten this thing out, go ahead and spill it. Let's hear it."

"Well, there's just one thing I can say — I wasn't there."

"But can you prove that?" asked Captain Wilson.

"Yes, I can prove it. When I left this room Mary and I made a beeline for the bar. I felt and she felt we had a drink coming to us. It's our wedding day and we're not going to be able to get married and I've been dragged through all the muck and slime of this murder case, and I felt I had a drink coming to me. There weren't more than fifteen people in that bar. But they all know me and they all saw me and they will all swear I never left it till you yanked me out just now. And if that's not an alibi, Captain, how do you spell it?"

"It looks like an alibi," said the Captain. "But you could have slipped away for a minute."

"I could have," said Watson, "but I didn't. Perhaps you can explain how I could stand with Mary beside me, her arm through mine, and still commit a murder."

CHAPTER 15

WITH THE POLICE COMMISSIONER and Inspector Hunt backing his every move, Captain Wilson came to sudden disaster with his plan to keep the square isolated. The plan had been carefully worked out, the telephone wires had been cut, no one was allowed to enter or leave the square without permission. But a game small boys play smashed the whole scheme. The situation was written carefully on a piece of paper which was folded like a dart and thrown from the roof of a house, and it glided to the next street. It was a call for help, signed by ten men imprisoned in the square, and it brought the Mayor back to the improvised police station on the run.

With the doors locked and the window shades drawn, the Mayor, who never sat down, was standing by the table in the room, and with him was Commissioner Doyle, Inspector Hunt and Captain Wilson. And the time was midnight.

"There's just one thing you can do, Captain," said the Mayor. "Perhaps there is more than one, but there is one thing you can't do, and that is go on with this scheme. The minute that floating piece of paper was picked up, it found its way into the hands of Levy, Strassburger, Levy & Crowninshield, and you know who they and what they are. In the first place it's a good case, and for another thing it offers them some swell free advertising.

"And when court opens tomorrow at ten o'clock you'll find Crowninshield waiting for a court order. I've had the District Attorney with me for an hour, and we've been over it from every angle. Wilson, there's nothing to prevent you from arresting every man, woman and child in this place as material witnesses, as suspects, as accomplices, or anything else you like, but you would have to lock them up. And you'd have to bring them into court or you can turn them all out."

"This murderer is going to be caught," said Wilson.

"How?" asked the Mayor.

"In a trap. If it's the last act of my life."

"And how are you going to do that?" asked Hunt.

"That," said Wilson, "is something I haven't worked out yet, but I will. I'll set a trap for him, I'll bait it, and I'll spring it if he falls for the trap. And I think he will fall for it. That's all.

"That's all. Catch him the way they catch tigers in India. There are two ways of doing that. One way is for the hunter to sit up on the head of an elephant with two gun bearers back of him and with beaters running through the jungle to try and scare out a tiger. That's one way. But there is a surer way than that. In the first place you have no gun bearers. Just one gun and you. And you climb a tree late at night, toward morning, almost. And there you sit quietly. And underneath the tree you have tethered a young goat and naturally the young goat tethered and unable to get away commences to bleat. And the soft night air carries the sound of that bleating for miles. And finally the tiger hears it. And the bleating of a goat always makes a tiger hungry. So he starts towards the breakfast while you sit up in the tree and you wait and you wait. You strain your eyes in the jungle and underbrush, and you don't see anything and don't hear anything. Not a sound. And then suddenly, out of nowhere, seemingly, a long, lean, striped thing comes through the early dawn. It's your tiger come for his breakfast, and that's when you kill him."

"And how," asked the Mayor, "are you going to bring all this about?"

"I don't know exactly," said Wilson.

"And this man's name?" said the Mayor, after a long pause.

"If you don't mind, sir, I think not," said Captain Wilson. "Just for the moment it's his secret and it's mine."

Evanhoe joined Wilson a few minutes after the Mayor and Doyle left. The Captain went over to the table that served as a desk and wrote a name on a piece of paper and handed it to him. Evanhoe read it and whistled. Then he came closer to the Captain and said: "What about him?"

"I want him tailed," said the Captain. "I want four men on the job under you. Pick him up when he leaves his house, and I want you to put him to bed at night. Use as many men as you like — I want four men anyhow — and here is the way you'll work it out. He knows you?"

"Yes."

"Then you must keep out of his sight. I want one man not more than twenty feet back of him all the time. And you can change your man as often as you like. But don't let that killer suspect that he is being followed. Naturally you'll all be in plain clothes. If he stops and talks to a girl or a woman, your men move in. They must not be more than two or three feet away from him then, and ready to shoot. I think, Evanhoe, that after you have given your instructions you'd better stay here. I'll be back in a little while. I'll want reports every half-hour from the men following this man. That's your layout. First comes the suspect, then your policeman in plain clothes, and back of him another policeman in plain clothes, and when the first is sent away on an errand or to telephone me, the man back of him moves up to take his place."

By seven o'clock the next morning the square had resumed its normal aspect. No policemen around, except two or three standing outside the room Wilson was still using. Men from the telephone company were repairing wires, children were getting ready for school, and Wilson, now alone in his temporary office, was walking up and down the floor.

Later that day as Captain Wilson walked toward his apartment house for lunch he ran into Gus Smith, the postman. Smith was out of uniform and so was the Captain. Wilson came up behind Smith and put his hand on his shoulder very quietly.

"Well, Gus," said the Captain, "what are you doing up in this neighborhood?"

Smith grinned at him. "It's my day off," he said. "As a matter of fact, I wanted to see you, Captain. I've got sort of an idea I would like to talk over with you."

"Now that's a funny thing," said Wilson, "I've been think-ing a lot about you too, Gus. I've been thinking you can help me on this case a lot. Have you had lunch?" he added.

"Why, no," said Smith, "not yet."

"Fine," said Wilson, "that's fine. I want you to meet my wife and my daughter."

"Oh, you got a daughter?"

"Have I? You ought to see her. Most beautiful girl in the world. Perfectly swell kid. Here we are," he said suddenly and turned into an apartment house.

"I don't know about this," said the postman. "It's pretty early in the day. Won't your wife be kind of fussy about com-pany she isn't expecting?"

"I'm the boss in my house. Come on in."

Mrs. Wilson met them in the hallway. "I met Gus Smith outside, my dear," the Captain said heartily, "and there are some things we have to talk over, so I thought we could have a cup of coffee."

"Don't you believe him, Mr. Smith," said Mrs. Wilson, with a laugh. "I've lived with him a thousand years and I've never seen him satisfied with a cup of coffee. Come in, and we'll see what we can find. Suppose we start with some strawberries and cream and buttered toast and maybe an omelette."

"That's the stuff," said Wilson. "Mother," he added, turn-ing to his wife, "Gus is in the postal service, and I just wanted to show him how much better a cop lives than a postman. Where's Martha?"

"She'll be round in a minute," said Mrs. Wilson. "She was up pretty late last night. She went out dancing with that young lieutenant of yours."

"That's fine," said Wilson, "fine. Dancing with a police-man, eh? That's all right as far as I'm concerned. Only she ought to remember there are other men in the world. We don't want our daughter out with policemen all the while."

"But I thought you said—"

"You must have misunderstood me," Wilson interrupted. "I have no objection to the young fellow, even though he is a cop. Come on, Gus, let's get something to eat." And they walked into the dining-room.

"Nice place you got here," said Smith, seating himself at the table.

"We like it," said Wilson. "We've been here a great many years. Martha was born here. We've all been very happy here together. It's a funny thing, Smith; everything's been going along fine, year after year. Getting nearer to the time for me to retire and take my pension, and then suddenly I'm hit with the biggest trouble I've ever had since I've been in the department—the only serious trouble I've had, as a matter of fact."

"Yes, I know. It's terrible, terrible," said the postman. "I read that editorial in the paper, and it was pretty dirty. Haven't you any idea who it could be, Captain?"

"Not an idea in the world. That fellow is too smart for me. That's why I wanted to talk to you, Gus. You get around—go places I don't. I want you to keep your ears open and tip me off to anything you hear. And here is one thing I want to tell you, but I don't want it to get around. The Mayor was up at our little office in the square last night and he gave me hell. He says the murders have got to stop or I'll have to get out."

"But that's not fair," said Gus. "You've done your work, and just because you've run up against a fellow who's smarter than you are—smarter than all the cops, it looks like—what makes him think of getting rid of you?"

"Gus, the man who's doing these murders has got a grudge against me. He says if I lose my job, if I'm kicked out and so on, he'll quit killing young girls."

"Why, he must hate you."

"Yes, I guess he does."

"It's terrible for you, Captain. I hope he don't find out you got a daughter. My God, that's an awful thought, isn't it? Why, if this fellow found out you had a daughter he might decide he'd kill her!"

"Yes, I know," said Wilson. "Well, probably he'll never find out I've got a daughter. How would he know about her?"

"Captain, haven't you any idea who the killer is?"

"My God, Gus, I'm going crazy trying to think who it could be."

"Well, all I can say is, it's the most mysterious case I've ever heard of. Of course, like everybody else, I've been think-ing about it. I thought at first it was that young doctor fellow. But he's got an alibi—in that last case, anyhow. He couldn't have killed Goldie. Look, Captain: could the killer be a trained nurse? They know how to use a knife pretty near as good as a doctor, don't they?"

"Now, that's an idea," said Wilson. "I hadn't thought of that. A woman, huh?"

"Well, is there anybody else, Captain, would know how to use a knife like that but a doctor or a trained nurse?"

"I can't think of anyone," said the Captain.

Then Martha joined them—a Martha lovely, gay, and laughing.

CHAPTER 16

GUS SMITH WAS ON HIS WAY OUT. An hour had passed most pleasantly. He had shaken hands with Mrs. Wil-son and now he came with outstretched hand toward Martha. Her father had risen and was standing beside his daughter. He had thrown one arm across her shoulder and drawn her closer to him.

Smith said: "Well, goodbye, Miss Martha."

"Goodbye. We've enjoyed having you here. Father doesn't often bring his friends in for lunch."

"I certainly enjoyed it," said Smith. "It was a nice meal. And that's a fine girl you've got, Captain. A fine girl. Well, goodbye; I'll have to be stepping along."

As the door closed, the girl turned and looked sharply at her father. "Pop, what's the matter with you? Mom, come and look at the old man, he's having a chill or something."

Mrs. Wilson, who had left the room, came running back. She put her hand quickly to her husband's forehead. "You're wringing wet, what's the matter?"

"Nothing. I'll be all right in a minute. It's nothing." Then for a minute he lost control of himself. "By God," he shouted, "they can't ask this of me! Police work is police work. But they can't ask this."

Martha came closer to her father. "What scared you, Pop? What did that man do that scared you?"

"Nothing, nothing at all, Martha. What did you do with that little automatic pistol I gave you once? Where did you put it?"

"I don't know. It's somewhere in my bureau. Why do you want it?"

"Go and get it."

As the girl ran out of the room her mother came closer to the Captain. "What is it?" she asked.

"It's not anything, but I've got to tell you. I've got to tell you, and if you want to take a rolling pin and bat me over the head with it, why go on and do it. I've got it coming to me." Then he said slowly: "Either I'm entirely on the wrong track or that fellow is one of three men who could have killed these girls."

"And you brought him here? You let him sit there looking at our daughter?"

"Yes. I had to."

"You wanted him to know you had a daughter?"

"Yes."

"The idea being," she went on, "that if he is the man he'll try to kill her? You'll have to answer that question, you know."

"Yes, that's the idea."

"And what's going to happen to you and me if he does?"

"Well, my dear, if he kills Martha, it won't matter much what happens to you and me. But we're not going to let him do that."

And for the first time since they were married, Mrs. Wilson said a cruel thing to her husband: "You've let him kill a good many other girls. How could you do it! How could you do it! If all the things you've told me about the others are true, and if this is the murderer and he knows we have a girl, it's the one thing he'll want to do."

"Yes, it's the one thing he'll want to do. He won't bother any other girl from now on. All his thoughts will be on my kid, and how he'll kill her."

"And you still say you don't know why he's doing this?"

"No, I haven't the faintest idea. And I haven't any evidence that he has killed anybody."

Martha came running in. The little pistol proved to be a flat, short-nosed, ugly-looking .38 automatic.

"Here it is, Pop," she said. "What will I do with it?"

"I want you to carry it for a few days. I don't suppose there is any place in these new clothes you're wearing where you could put it, is there?"

"No, there isn't. But why must I carry this thing?" She gave a little cry. "Pop, that's the man, is it? That funny little man? That's the one who's been killing all those girls?"

"I think perhaps it is."

"And you brought him here to see me?"

"Yes, he did," said her mother. "And I'm never going to forgive him. He hadn't any right—"

"Wait a minute, sister," said Martha. "Wait a minute. I want to think this out. Yes, he had a right, Mother. I can see that. Mother, don't you see that a cop is just as much a soldier as a soldier is, every bit? Pop has had his orders to catch this man, and if he's right in what he thinks, I'm the bait. Is that it, Father?"

"Yes, that's it."

"Don't you see, Mother, he had to do it."

"No, I don't see anything of the kind."

"I tried to tell her," began the Captain.

"Yes, I know, Pop, but let me tell her."

"What would you know about it?" asked her mother.

"Oh, well, I've got brains, I can think these things out. Pop has been a policeman all his life. He started by pounding the pavements and worked his way up, and now he's a captain and next thing you know he'll be an inspector."

"That's not it at all," said the Captain.

"You must let me explain this to Mother in my own way, please. A captain has to set an example for his men, Mother. I don't mean just the men under him; I mean every man of the department of a lower rank than he is—and maybe some of a higher rank. Pop has orders to get this man, and I'm scared, I'm scared to death, but we're going to do it, aren't we, Pop, you and I? We're going to get him. And I have a feeling that he won't—he won't hurt me."

"Hurt you?" said her father. "Good God, when he sat at that table, that was as near as he'll ever get to you. That's what I wanted you to get the pistol for. I want you to promise that he's never to get closer than ten feet to you—never again. Keep that gun with you and if he comes near you kill him, just as you would a mad dog. Now where can you carry that thing? Have you got a pocket? Have you got anything?"

"In pictures and stories they strap it around their leg. But skirts are so short this year."

"How about a bertha?" said her mother.

"What the hell is a bertha?" asked the Captain.

Martha gave a little cry of delight. "Mother, that will do it. Wait a minute, Pop." She was laughing as she ran out of the room. In a minute she returned, fastening around her throat a very lovely cloth. It might have been chiffon, but it was heavier. This she tucked into her belt, then with a smile at her father she picked up her automatic and slipped it inside of this.

"I look demure and innocent, don't I?" she asked.

Her father was not in the mood for pleasantries. "Let's see how quick you can get it into your hand."

There was a flashing movement of the girl's right hand, then she cried, "Stick 'em up," and the automatic was in her hand and ready for use.

"That's my girl," said the Captain, "that's the way to do

it.'' And he kissed her. And then shook his head slowly.

"Now listen, you two," he said. "I'm not quite the skunk I seem to be. And I don't think Martha is really in any danger. But I've got to be sure—I've got to be sure. Now you understand, daughter, if he comes to within ten feet and you're not being protected by me or another policeman, you kill him. Don't try to hit him in the face or any nonsense like that at all."

"I know. Right in the stomach."

"Well, it's easier to hit. But shoot straight at him. You can't miss him at ten feet—and a .38 bullet pumped into his stomach will fix him. Girls, I have to do this. Nobody knew what to do. Nobody had any plans. And I had to have a decoy that was sure, so there wouldn't be a failure."

Then the doorbell rang. As Mrs. Wilson started toward it, the Captain stopped her. "I'll attend to that, and from now on we're going to have a butler here. And he'll answer the doorbell and he'll answer the telephone calls. I expect," he said to his daughter, "you'd like that same cop that's so stuck on you."

"Yes, I would. And, incidentally, Pop, I'm stuck on him."

Captain Wilson came back a few minutes later with a young man; slim, short, smooth-shaven—dapper would be the word for him.

"This," said the Captain, "is Tommy Harrigan. He's an old friend of mine—he's a cop and he isn't a cop. He's not large enough to be a cop and he's too smart not to be one."

"What your father means, Miss Martha," said Tom, "is that I'm an undercover guy, and if there is a tough job to be done, I do it, and nobody knows about it at all. Now, then, Cap, what do you want?"

"I told you. There she is. Anything doing?"

"I can do most of it, I think," said Tom. "I don't think I can do the voice. Would you say something, please, Miss Martha?"

"I don't know what you mean. Do you want me to recite or just talk?"

"Well, let's hear you talk to your father. Call him Dad, or Pop, or whatever it is. And then talk to your mother."

So the girl said: "Well, Dad" and "Well, Molly" and "Well, Mr. Harrigan."

And the boy laughed at her and said: "That will do. I don't suppose you have ever acted much, have you?"

"Why, no. Not on the stage."

"Well, let's try, then. Suppose you have a cold, a terrible cold. You're so hoarse you can hardly talk at all. Let's hear that."

Martha, still bewildered, cried: "Hello, Pop; Hello, Mom. How's that Mr. Harrigan?"

And almost in the same voice, Harrigan came back with: "That's fine, Miss Martha; that's fine."

"Well, for the land's sake!" said Mrs. Wilson.

"Now," said her father, "let's see you walk across the room and come running back to me."

The girl did it.

Young Harrington had no trouble in imitating her at all. Martha began to laugh. "I know what it is," she said. "He's going to be me. He's going to be me."

"Sure," said the boy, "and I'll give you a good show too. Now, Captain, if I could have one of her dresses, the one she's going to wear tonight."

"But you couldn't get into one of my dresses," said Martha.

"No, I couldn't. I'm little but I'm not that little. But I could have one made exactly like it. And I want a photograph of you, and a hat—the hat you'll be wearing tonight."

Martha ran out of the room to get the hat and the dress, and Mrs. Wilson looked at the boy for a minute. "Young fellow, you're taking an awful risk, you know that?"

"That's what he's being paid for," said her husband.

"Yes," said Harrigan, "that's what I'm getting paid for. I get money out of it and I get a lot of fun out of it."

"It wouldn't be any fun," said Mrs. Wilson, "if that man sticks his knife into your heart."

"No, that wouldn't be fun. I can see that. But if he tried it, what do you think I'd be doing all the time? Standing there and pointing to my heart and saying: 'This is the place'? Don't worry about me, Mrs. Wilson; I'm taking care of myself.''

Then Martha brought in the dress and the hat, and the boy looked at them and grinned as he packed them into a box. ''I might squeeze into it at that.''

''Don't you try it,'' said Martha. ''That's a new frock.''

The Captain's manner was almost fatherly as he faced Harrigan. ''Son, you'll have to step on it. I want that hat and dress back here by five o'clock tonight.''

''Oh, sure. That's nothing. My mother will run it up in no time. Well,'' he said, going toward the door, ''I'll be seeing you.''

As the door closed the Captain spoke again, this time more seriously. ''Daughter, this is not a joke, and it's not a game. I'll have a policeman round here to take care of you in a few minutes.''

''You needn't bother, Father. I've got one of my own.''

''I thought,'' said Wilson, ''I'd get this fellow Casey to come up and take care of you. I'll call up his station house and have his captain send him over right away.''

''You needn't bother. Today is his day off and he's on his way here now.''

''Holy smoke!'' said the Captain. ''You were out with him last night and now he's coming round here again.''

''Yes. He seems to like being with me.''

The Captain came closer to his daughter. ''Is it serious, kid?''

''Yes, Father,'' she said very quietly, ''it's serious. We were going to keep it secret for a little while, but it isn't any use.''

''You mean the guy wants to marry you?''

''I mean we want to marry each other. Here he comes now.''

''I don't hear anything.''

''You don't? You're not listening at the right place. Come here.'' And she dragged his face closer to her breast. ''Hear it now? That's love." And the door bell rang.

The Captain walked toward the door. "If it's Casey it'll be his job to answer the door for the rest of the day." He opened the door, and when Casey saw his superior officer he had the grace to blush a little.

"Come in," said the Captain. "I was just going to send for you."

Martha swaggered past her father and kissed her young man on the lips.

"My God!" said the Captain.

"And why not?" said his wife.

"I was going to speak to you about it today, Captain," said the red-faced young lieutenant.

"It'll do no good now," said the Captain. "She has told me everything." He grinned and added: "And it's all right as far as I'm concerned. And I want to say this much now. It was fine we had this little bit of fun-making as you came in, because I don't think there is going to be much laughter for a little while. We must get this man, and I don't mean tomorrow or the next day. And I've made my plans for that. And I've done something that I think most people would say I was crazy for—and maybe I was. I brought a man who, I think, may be doing these murders up here a little while ago, so he could see Martha, so he would think of nothing else but killing her."

"And what," asked Casey, "will I be doing all that time?"

"You," said the Captain, "will be taking care of her for me today. That's all you have to do. I want you to bring her down to the little place in the square where we have been for the last few days, about five o'clock this afternoon. I'm glad you're not in uniform. It's much better that way. And after she leaves the house with you nobody is to speak to her."

CHAPTER 17

A LITTLE LATER, AT POLICE HEADQUARTERS, Commissioner Doyle and Inspector Hunt still sat in easy chairs listening to the news broadcast coming to them: "It is now two seconds before four o'clock, and this is the city's own station. This broadcast comes to you as a public service. It gives us great pleasure to bring you the words of the Mayor himself at this time."

Doyle looked at Hunt and grinned. "You could gamble that the little fellow wouldn't miss a trick like that."

Then the barking voice of the Mayor. "Fellow Americans, and, above all, the mothers of this great city. I want to re-assure you that the frightful murders that have been taking place here are about to stop. We must have every faith in our police department. It is the greatest in the world. I know that you will say: 'What about all these murders? What about all these girls that have been killed?' And all I can say to you is that conditions have been unprecedented and the work the police have done has been endless. But I can promise you that after today there will be no more murders. So my advice to you is this: Stay at home. Don't open your door unless you know who is outside. Keep your daughters at home, no mat-ter what their plans are for the rest of the day. Keep them home. And that's all I can tell you. Keep your daughters home, keep your doors locked, keep your faith in the police of this great city, and wait patiently for tomorrow."

"So what?" said Hunt as he looked at Doyle.

"So the Mayor has spoken."

"And we hear nothing from Wilson," said Hunt. "What's he doing? What's he planning? He said he didn't want any help. Now he does. Wants me back in that little square that we tried to turn into a prison—and didn't."

They turned their attention to the radio again. "This is the city's own station. At the request of his honor, the Mayor, we ask people to turn to this station at five o'clock this afternoon. There will be a broadcast from the now well-known room used by the police as Little Headquarters in Greenwood Square, where two of these murders have taken place. Our own reporters will be there and will broadcast the plans of the police. For the first time in the history of the city you will have a complete insight into the way the police department of this city works. You will be allowed to sit in, practically, on the effort made to arrest the murderer of these girls. Don't forget to tune in at five o'clock."

Wilson and Evanhoe were waiting to spring the trap. They were back in the square, in the room commandeered for police use. Wilson was fidgety. He sat still for a minute, then he got up and walked round the room. Then he sat down again.

"Nervous?" said Evanhoe.

"Scared to death. I shouldn't have done it."

"It's not too late to change."

"Yes, it is. And there is nothing else I can do. This thing can't go on, and I don't know of any other way to stop it. Come in," he said as someone knocked on the door. Young Harrigan came in carrying a suitcase.

"Well," said the Captain, "what about it?"

Harrigan grinned at him. "I'm ready as soon as you are. I'm the prettiest girl you ever saw, I'll tell you that."

And at that moment the door opened and a squad of six policemen came in. The smallest was six foot two, and as they spread out Martha Wilson was disclosed. She had been in the center of this mob of cops.

"Now, Tommy," said Wilson, "run into the next room and change. I don't know how soon this thing is going to start."

As Harrigan turned away Martha called after him: "How do you look? Honestly, how do you look?"

"Like your twin—only more beautiful."

"I like your nerve." And she laughed gaily. She was trying very hard not to let her father see how scared and nervous she was.

Then Wilson turned toward his daughter. "Come here. I don't suppose there's anyone in the city that wouldn't have a hard word for me because of what I'm doing tonight.''

''I never had a hard word for you in my life.''

''And you haven't now?''

''Of course not. I know what you have to do, and I know how you have to do it. It's nothing very strange for an army officer to order his own son to do dangerous things, is it? But what I don't see, what I don't understand, is how you're going to get him to come here. Suppose it's someone you haven't even suspected yet. How are you going to tell him I'm here, and here is his big chance to hurt you?''

''That's a problem, isn't it?''

And, as if on a cue in a play, the door opened and in trooped men with cables, microphones, reflectors and other implements for a broadcast. And after them clumped Inspector Hunt. There was nothing of worry showing in his demeanor. He came over promptly and kissed Martha's cheek, chucked her under the chin and said: ''Hello, beautiful.''

And Martha kissed the old man very tenderly and said: ''Darling, it's nice to see you again.''

And then the broadcaster cut in on the conversation: ''It's after four o'clock, and we're supposed to be on the air at five. You'd better get ready. I'll have to hear all these voices. Let's take the young lady first.''

And he sat down at a side table and put on earphones and watched the dial on an oblong box filled with indicators that had knobs on it, a thing called a monitor.

''Now, Miss Wilson,'' he said, ''if you'll speak into that microphone we'll get some sort of register of your voice.''

''Wait a minute,'' said Wilson. ''She's supposed to have a very bad cold and she can barely speak.''

''Oh,'' said the broadcaster, ''I didn't know that. Well, we can fix that. All right, Miss Wilson, say anything you like.''

Martha assumed a hoarseness which was not hers and came close to the mike and said: ''I'm sorry I can't say anything because I've got such a bad cold.''

''You'd better try that again,'' said the radio expert, ''that's too clear.''

Martha tried it again, and the man turned the knob again and her voice was distorted—very hoarse and almost impossible to understand. He grinned at her and waved her from the mike. He took off his earphones and said: "That was fine, Miss Wilson, fine." Martha asked in her clear, young voice: "Is that the way you wanted it?"

"Yes, exactly. Now, Cap, what about the other one?"

"Yes, we'd better try him," said Wilson. "Come on in, Tommy," he called.

As the door opened and Harrigan came into the room Martha screamed. And well she might. There was Tommy; a little taller than she, made up to look exactly like her, same frock, same hat, stride a little longer maybe. He winked at her. "What did I tell you, kid. Your twin—only better looking."

"Okay," said the expert, "let's try it."

And then Tommy did his stuff. His voice was as hoarse and as inarticulate as the girl's. "I have this terrible cold," he said. "I can hardly talk at all. I'm very sorry because my father wanted me to talk to you."

And as he finished Martha said slowly under her breath: "Well, I'll be darned."

"And now," said Wilson, "for our information, let's hear you scream, Tommy; a scream that you can't get out—a choke of fright, rather."

And Tommy did that too. A half-choked cry, a gurgle, then a whimpering breathlessness of fright.

Then he cleared his throat and said quite naturally: "Well, how was that?"

"That," said the Captain, "was perfect."

CHAPTER 18

A TALL, LANTERN-JAWED young man suddenly threw his cigar away, looked at his watch, and jumped to his feet.

"It's ten minutes to five, gentlemen," he said. "You realize, of course, that anything that is said in here while we're on the air will be picked up. We have had one rehearsal, and I think that is enough."

Mrs. Durkin sat looking out of her window overlooking the square. This time she was not alone. Mrs. Schultz was with her. And Goldie Newmark's sister, who had come over from New Jersey. And two other women. They were talking in whispers. Mrs Schultz kept saying: "Is it five o'clock yet? Is it five o'clock yet?" And then it became five o'clock suddenly, and old Mrs. Durkin reached out a plump and somewhat grimy hand and turned a knob. The room was filled with sound:

"To the seven million people of Greater New York we are sending, by order of His Honor the Mayor, a complete broadcast of certain police proceedings having to do with Captain Wilson's efforts to solve the mystery of the recent series of murders of young girls in Manhattan. This broadcast is unrehearsed, and what you will hear is a word-for-word broadcast of the happenings in a room facing Greenwood Square, the square in which two young girls were killed within the last thirty-six hours. It now gives me great pleasure to introduce to you Conrad Galbraith, the famous commentator. Take it away, Mr. Galbraith."

And then a masculine voice: "Galbraith speaking. We are doing here today something never before attempted on the air. We are sitting now in an unfurnished room in which Captain Wilson and his men have been working for days. It has none of the conveniences and appurtenances of an office at Police Headquarters. There are telephones, the microphone from which I am speaking, two tables and five or six kitchen chairs, and half a dozen men with brains and experience. Experts with all the mental equipment that has made the police department of New York City what it is today, the finest in the world. I want to explain to you that this broadcast is allowed because it was first suggested by His Honor the Mayor, of this great city, and then approved by the Police

Commissioner himself, who is in his office in Centre Street, downtown, listening to every word that is spoken here. I now give way to Captain Wilson who will speak to you.''

Then came Captain Wilson's voice. There was a new note in it, a serene sort of a note. He no longer seemed frightened or anxious. On the contrary, he seemed very sure of himself. He spoke with a measured tone: ''Citizens of the greatest city in America. You have been invited to listen to the broadcast from this small room because both the Police Commissioner and His Honor the Mayor want you to discover for yourselves how the police are working and what methods they are using. I don't have to tell you what these murders have meant to me. There have been so many we have almost lost count of them. Young girls stabbed through the heart, and the murderer disappearing and leaving no clue. At the present moment I can truthfully say that I do not know who committed these murders. There are three men here in this little square who might have done it. Each has been suspected, and while none of them has been arrested, all three of them are now outside the door waiting to talk to me. They have been questioned from time to time. But no evidence has been brought forth that would warrant my making an arrest. These men will all be examined again and questioned again, and I want you to listen carefully to what they say. Try and put yourself in my place. Now,'' went on the Captain, ''I will talk to James Hooper.''

''So,'' Hooper was shouting, ''you're bringing me back again, are you?''

''Come up here by the table,'' said Wilson.

Hooper's voice rose still higher. ''I'm coming when I please, going where I please, and doing what I please. I've got a bellyful of you cops already.''

''Evanhoe,'' said Wilson.

''Take your hands off me,'' yelled Hooper.

Then came the gruff tones of Evanhoe. ''Up there by the table, sucker, and step on it. We've got no time to waste.''

''Yes,'' said Hooper, ''and if I don't go, you'll beat me up again, just like you did before, won't you?''

"We will," said Evanhoe, "and worse. Get up there."

And then the measured tones of Wilson came in:

"You know, Hooper, you're not cleared at all of the killing of Minnie Schultz. We don't know enough about you yet. Who you are and where you came from. It's not clear at all. You say you had the record of that violin solo as a lesson, and we say you had it as an alibi. And you ran that record to make us believe you were up in your room playing your fiddle. What you got to say to that?''

"What I said before. Just what I said before. I wasn't out of my room, and I was working with my violin. And it's no use going through this thing again and again this way. This is a free country, this is America. I was born here and no cop has the right to treat me the way you're treating me. And before we get through this I'm going to have the coat off your back—yes, and your brass buttons—and to hell with you.''

Very quietly the Captain's voice came through again: "But you can't prove that you didn't run up the stairs and over the roof and down the cellar and kill Minnie Schultz, can you?''

"I don't have to prove it," shouted Hooper. "I know enough about the law to know that I am innocent till you prove me guilty, and you can't do that. What would I kill her for?''

"And then there is Goldie Newmark," went on the Captain. "You remember Goldie Newmark. You took a drink with her. It was only yesterday. Now she's gone. And she was killed by a man wearing a gray coat. Now, Hooper, why did you hide your gray coat when we looked through your place? We got it at last, we found it.''

"That coat isn't mine," shouted Hooper. "I never had a gray coat.''

"What do you call that?" asked Captain Wilson.

The announcer's voice came in: "At this moment Captain Wilson is holding out his hand and in it is a gray coat. Listen to him.''

"What do you call that?" asked Captain Wilson. "That's a gray coat, isn't it?"

"It's not mine," said Hooper. "I didn't kill Goldie New-mark, I can tell you that. You're framing me, that's what you're doing, framing me, and I refuse to answer any more questions until I get a lawyer."

In his office in the City Hall, the Mayor was striding up and down. With him were the District Attorney and Police Commissioner Doyle.

"I wish I'd thought of it before," said the Mayor. "It's great stuff. If I had known it was going to be this good, I'd have made a nation-wide broadcast of it."

And then a new voice came over the air: "Excuse me, folks; I am Inspector Hunt, and I haven't said anything over the air yet. I just wanted you all to know I'm here, and want you to get used to the sound of my voice, because sometime I might have to say something because it's important. And now, stand-ing in the doorway here is one of the prettiest girls you ever saw. Her name is Mary Lester, and it's going to be that for two or three more hours. And standing beside her is Dr. Ray-mond Watson. And we are interested in him for a good many reasons. We're pretty sure that a doctor could have committed these murders better than anybody else. And he owns and runs a taxi which he used to drive around at night to pay his way through college. He could have gone all over the city and com-mitted these murders. And here he is now standing in the doorway with his girl. Let's hear what Captain Wilson has to say to him."

And then this came over the air:

"Come in, you two, and sit down. Well, Watson, what did you want to say to me?"

"Yesterday," said Watson, "I promised you I wouldn't leave this place without your knowing about it. Well, I want you to release me from that promise; and if you don't, then I'm going to break it. I'm going to get out of here. We thought we were going to be married yesterday."

Then another voice came in. "Friends, this is Inspector

Hunt speaking. The boy is right, Captain. I'm going to take these two young folks out and get them married and bring 'em back.''

Mrs. Durkin heard this too, and all the women with her. "Now that's a nice fellow, that Inspector," said Mrs. Durkin.

"Yes, sir, that will be quite a wedding, won't it? Church wedding, a priest, and I hope they'll have the boys singing too. It's beautiful to hear the boys sing. My wedding wasn't like that. Just me and the fellow and the justice of the peace and my dear papa. The main thing about weddings is, you can't make them binding but you can make them legal. Jesus! did you hear that door slam?" All the old women drew closer to the radio. Something was happening. Then Captain Wilson's voice came over the radio:

"Well, Inspector Hunt, you're not back already! They're not married, are they?"

"No, they're not. I sent Evanhoe with them to be the usher, best man, and the whole bag of tricks. Captain, I got a message for you—a message from the Mayor, okayed by Doyle. These murders have got to stop, says the Mayor; he won't give you the rest of the week he promised you; this is your last chance. If there's another girl killed by this fiend, out you go.''

Then came the announcer's voice again:

"Captain Wilson is standing now close beside the radio. I've asked him if he has any statement to make, and he refuses to speak again. His face is flushed with anger. He says he has nothing to say at this time. Keep tuned to this station. This broadcast will be resumed in a little while.''

CHAPTER 19

AN HOUR LATER, AT SIX O'CLOCK, the news broadcast on the murder mysteries was resumed. Some two million persons were listening in, but was the murderer among them?

At a signal from the broadcaster, the door was slammed, and the man who did it was waved back to his seat. Captain Wilson and Martha approached the microphone, and Wilson said: "Martha, Martha, what are you doing down here?" Then he stepped back to make way for Martha, who came close to the mike. You could hardly hear her voice, it was so hoarse. "Mother was so frightened," she said, "she wanted me down here with you. She knew I'd be safe with you. You told her to send me down here if she got afraid for me."

The radio man pointed a finger at Wilson, giving him the cue for his next speech. Wilson said: "What's the matter with your voice? You can hardly speak."

And again Martha came close to the mike and said: "I've got a cold. I can hardly talk at all, Daddy."

Then the grinning Hunt lumbered toward the mike and his voice boomed out: "Captain, how dared you do this? Your own daughter! You know she has been threatened by this man. You know that almost no girl is safe away from home! And you tell your wife to send her down here where two girls have been killed within a few hours of each other! How dared you do this?"

Then Wilson was back by the microphone and his voice came out strong and vibrant:

"Inspector, she's my daughter. I'm not afraid of this man and his threats. As a matter of fact, she's safer here with me than anywhere else. I know what you're trying to tell me. Because Martha has lost her voice, she can't cry for help in an emergency. Well, there won't be an emergency. I'll be right by her side all the time."

Thus the make-believe continued. And in the Mayor's office they were listening.

"This is as good as a show," said the Mayor. "I wonder how much of it is real and how much is make-believe?"

Suddenly Doyle said: "Did you hear that? Did you hear that one?"

"Yes, I heard it. Sounded like a postman's whistle."

And so the Mayor and the District Attorney and the Police

Commissioner continued to listen to the radio, and this is what they heard:

First a door slammed. Then Wilson speaking: "Well, well, what are you doing down here, Gus? I thought this was your day off. Too much mail for the other boys, I suppose."

"Yes, too much mail. They had to call me back on duty, and I'm even having to work after hours. There's nothing for you, Captain, but I saw the crowd as I was passing and wondered what was going on."

Then came Hunt's voice: "Lots of things are happening, Gus. Glad you're here. It's lots of fun. We're broadcasting about those murders. What you think about it?"

"I think it's wonderful. Hello, Miss Martha," he said pleasantly. "I'm glad to see you again."

Then came Wilson's voice: "Gus, you mustn't mind if she can't answer you. You know how these colds come on so suddenly. It's a germ, and she's lost her voice. She can't talk at all."

"Oh," said the postman, "that's too bad, isn't it?"

Then Hunt's voice boomed out: "It's just like a show, Gus; it's lots of fun. Did you ever talk over the air?"

Smith's rather high voice came back again on the same genial tone: "No, I never did."

The Mayor said: "That voice sounds familiar to me, but I can't place it. I wonder—"

"Wait a minute," said the Commissioner. "Let's wait a minute. Maybe he'll say something more."

The high-pitched voice continued: "Friends, this is pretty bad, isn't it? All these girls being killed this way. They asked me about it, as I get around so much, and they asked me to tell them anything I saw. I go everywhere, from place to place and house to house. I knew two of them. Little Goldie was kind of gay and amusing, and that poor little Schultz girl—honest, folks, I cried when they told me she was dead. I had a daughter once and if she'd lived she'd have been about as old as the little Schultz girl was. I'm nothing now but an old widower, wandering around with letters. I've got nothing to do with this broadcast or the police, except to wish them luck. I go around from place to place, and they know I would tell them about anything I hear. But they'd know about it almost as soon as I would. Well, Inspector Hunt, that's all I can say about it. You know all about it and how I'd like to help."

There was a short pause and Hunt's voice came over the air again: "The voice you've just heard was that of Gus Smith, of the Post Office Department, who has been delivering letters around here for years. We all know him and are all fond of him. He's a hard-working, swell guy. Thanks for dropping in, Gus."

And Smith's voice came back again: "That's all right, Inspector. I'll do anything I can." And then there was a curious break in his voice. "Goodbye all," he went on, "and goodbye, Miss Martha. I'll be seeing you."

CHAPTER 20

THREE HOURS HAD PASSED since the broadcast from Greenwood Square had been finished and the microphones taken from the room. Just around the corner a police car was parked and with it were four motorcycles. The driver was in the car and the motorcycle cops ready for work. And the driver of the police car was a massive, clean-cut police lieutenant named Casey. So it wasn't hard to guess what that car was destined to do. It was waiting to take Martha home.

The murderer? Captain Wilson and his staff were sure they knew where he was. There was the unoccupied furnished room directly over the police headquarters in the Greenwood Square building. Captain Wilson had previously used it for his dictaphone listeners. After the broadcast Evanhoe had said loudly that he was going up to make sure nothing had been left lying around up there. He went noisily up the stairs, threw open the door with a bang, walked heavily about the room for a few moments, and then came clumping downstairs again, leaving the door open behind him. A few minutes later, Evanhoe tiptoed quietly up half the flight until he could see the door of the furnished room. It was closed now.

The murderer was sitting in that room. He knew it was dangerous for him to be there, but he knew too that he was too clever for the police and that this was his real chance to destroy Captain Wilson. He was tired of standing, tired of waiting. It was quiet and peaceful there in the room and the time passed pleasantly enough for the man whose crimes had terrified the biggest city in the world.

So the time passed. Upstairs, in the room over Captain Wilson's headquarters, the murderer took the knife out from its hiding place and felt it tenderly from end to end. He wiped the blade with a handkerchief and slipped the knife back. It was dark in the room now. The murderer got up and tiptoed across and opened the door; not much, just so he could hear.

Though the murderer had cautiously tiptoed across the room, the old, dry floorboards had creaked under his weight. Directly underneath, Captain Wilson and Inspector Hunt, listening intently, could barely hear the creaking boards. Wilson beckoned to his daughter and took her by the hand. Then, from a suitcase, he lifted a long black cloak and slipped it over the girl's clothing. And he put on her head a hat covered with a widow's veil. Then he kissed his daughter and said: "Run along home to your mother, darling. The Inspector will take you around the corner and there's a young cop named Casey waiting to take you home. You know the one I mean—the fellow who's been kissing you all the time."

Martha flushed and looked as little like a widow as anyone very well could. "Tell your mother," the Captain went on, "that I'll be home a little later on. And tell her I said you were a good, brave girl."

"Yes, Pop."

Under the protection of Inspector Hunt, Martha tiptoed out of the room, but, instead of going out of the front door, they went through the basement, out of the basement door into the square, and hurriedly disappeared around the corner.

Then Evanhoe came into the room, and he and the Captain talked for, a minute in whispers. Then young Harrigan appeared out of a back room. And now that Martha was gone, he looked still more like her.

As the three men talked in whispers, the floorboards of the room upstairs creaked again. With a nod Evanhoe tiptoed out of the room, down the long hallway, past the stairway which dropped steeply from the floor above, and out into the square, leaving the front door open. Captain Wilson and young Harrigan stood quietly waiting for a signal. And in spite of the fact that this signal had been planned and rehearsed quietly before, when it came it was to them like a clap of thunder. From out in the square came a scream: "Help! Help! Police! Police! Captain Wilson!"

Then Wilson and Harrigan went quickly into the hall and Wilson took up his cue.

"Daughter," he said, "I have to leave you for a minute. You heard them yelling for me! I must leave you for a minute. We've been through the house and there's no one in it. I'll leave the door open behind me, and if there's anything that frightens you in here, you come running. They're yelling for me out there. It must be another murder."

Harrigan said nothing, and the play went on. Wilson continued: "Your cold is worse, Martha. We must see a doctor about it. Why, you can't talk at all." And then he went noisily out into the street.

Instead of going back into the room, Harrigan moved a little further into the hallway. There was a full-length mirror on the wall and this reflected his slightly girlish figure, and also the stairway. The boards creaked twice, and Harrigan took a deep breath and stood looking in the mirror.

And then, down the stairs from the floor above, came two gray-clad legs. Instead of tightening his muscles and growing tense, Harrington did what all athletes do before a strain. He relaxed completely. And, as the mirror showed more and more of the figure of the man coming toward him, Harrington set himself for the death battle he knew was coming.

Now the postman was on the ground floor. Laughing a little, he said: "Well, well, Miss Martha, how is the cold?"

Harrington shook his head and did not turn.

"Let's take a look at your throat; maybe I can suggest something for it." He came a step nearer, and then, seeing that the street door was open, he moved quickly and closed and locked it softly. Then he eased his mailbag to the floor and from its bottom braces drew out his knife.

All these moves Harrigan had seen in the mirror, but still he stood before it as if entranced by the sight of himself.

The postman moved to within two feet of the figure at the mirror. "I guess," he said, "this will just about finish your father, the devil." Then he sprang for the kill. Harrigan moved too. Something exploded. It was the boy's hard fist, smashing to the point of Smith's jaw. The knife flew upward and fell, point down, on the floor. It stood upright quivering like a slender, wind-blown flower.

Harrigan let him get to his feet, and then smashed his fist into Smith's face. The postman screamed with pain, and lurched forward blindly. A left hook lifted him off his feet and dropped him to the floor. Harrigan stood over him a moment, and then stepped to the street door and uplocked it. Wilson, Evanhoe, and a half-dozen others streamed in.

And after that the first man to make a move was Hunt. He walked over to Wilson and slapped him on the back.

"You don't need me any more," he said. "I'm too old for this kind of thing, broadcasting on the air and then sitting in on a case like this, and arranging for the wedding of a young couple. Is there anything more I can do for you, Captain?"

"Yes," said the Captain, "there is. Call up the Commissioner and say we've got our man, and that I'm bringing him downtown."

"Well," said Captain Wilson to Gus Smith, "are you going to talk?"

"No."

"All right, it's not necessary." He pointed suddenly to the

knife on the floor. "There's the knife that killed all those girls,
and the handle is covered with your fingerprints. You were all
set to kill my daughter, and if I did what I wanted to I'd
stand you up there in front of me and hit you till my hands
bled. And then I'd start kicking you. I'm not going to do
that but, by God, you're going to talk."

"Like hell I am."

"Bring him out! Bring him out! Bring him out!" It was
like a chant, the voices of the women in wild rising chorus out
in the square. The old women of the neighborhood, called by
Mrs. Durkin to help the mothers of the murdered girls to their
vengeance.

"We want that man! We want that man!"

Wilson dragged Smith to a window and showed him the
crowded street.

A hundred hands stretched out to take him, countless voices
screamed at him.

"You know what they'll do to you! You'd better talk."

Smith talked. Words and profanities streamed from his
battered mouth; he drooled blood and he spat as the words
tumbled out.

"You probably say you don't remember me but you're a
liar," he cried. "I was doing nobody any harm and you — yes,
you, you dirty stinking cop, backed your horse into me. I
wasn't doing any harm. I was watching a parade, and for that
I was lame all the rest of my life, limping for thirty years up
and down the streets. I was going to be all sorts of fine things:
I was going to have a wife and a family; I was going to be rich.
But a lame man couldn't do the things I'd set out to do. It
took me four years to find out who had ridden over me. Remember the day your horse fell dead under you? I did that!
I poisoned your horse. I heard you cried about it — Christ,
didn't I laugh about that! Then my head bothered me, and
they put me away for a few years. A few years with a lot of
crazy men; but nothing bad happened to you. They made you
a sergeant of detectives. I was in the asylum when I heard
about that. I was out and looking for a job that a lame man

could do when they made you a lieutenant. Then I got so I could walk better, and I got a job in the post office.

"After I'd been a postman a while I saw a way to get even with you. A postman can go anywhere; nobody pays any attention to a postman. I read that in a book; I read how a postman in England, dressed in his uniform, carried the body of a girl he had killed right past the cops who were looking for the girl and the man who had killed her. He had the cut-up body of the girl in his mailbag, hanging over his shoulder.

"And when I read that, my head stopped aching; I saw my way out. I bought a bicycle to help me get around better. A lot of postmen use bicycles. I read books about murders all the time and I found out how to kill girls without letting them bleed all over me and how to write the Commissioner what I wanted him to know about you, you lousy devil, without giving myself away. I learned to make my voice sound wild over the phone so it wouldn't be recognized and so you'd think I was a crazy man. And it all worked, I'll tell the world it worked.

"I got a lot of girls, and you got more and more trouble. But I didn't know till the other day that you had a girl of your own. I was going to stop after killing her, for I knew you'd be no good after that." Smith was screaming now.

Out in the square the women too were screaming. "Bring him out! Bring him out! Bring him out!"

Police training is police training. Smith was taken through the square and downtown, surrounded by men in uniform. Despite their screaming and pushing, the women could not get at him.

Later that night Wilson said to his wife: "I couldn't turn him loose in that crowd of maniacs."

"I don't see why not," said his wife.

END